D1030340

Winter's Tales 23

Winter's Tales 23

edited by
Peter Collenette

ST. MARTIN'S PRESS
New York

All rights reserved.   For information, write:
St. Martin's Press, Inc., 175 Fifth Ave., New York, N.Y. 10010
Printed in Great Britain
Library of Congress Catalog Card Number: 77-10374
First published in the United States of America in 1978
ISBN: 0-312-88411-7

Contents

Acknowledgements

The stories are copyright respectively

© 1977 Southmoor Serendipity
© 1977 Anita Desai
© 1977 Geoffrey Household
© 1977 Peter Kemp
© 1977 Derwent May
© 1977 Rudolf Nassauer
© 1977 Catherine Rocks
© 1977 Nigel Gray
© 1977 James Stern
© 1977 Fay Weldon

Fred Scott's 'The Rescue Brigade' has been published in *Fireweed* in 1975.

Editor's Note

Compiling *Winter's Tales* has been fun, and the hardest part is writing the Editor's Note. Anyone, including me, searching for a common theme in this volume faces a problem, because as usual the choice was dictated by quirks of editorial taste. My thanks go to Alan Maclean for giving me the chance to indulge mine.

All but one of the authors represented here are new to *Winter's Tales* (the exception is Brian Aldiss). In particular, it is good to be introducing two brand-new writers of fiction, Peter Kemp and Catherine Rocks, whose talents are very different and very clear; and perhaps I should draw attention to the inclusion of Fred Scott's non-fictional oral reminiscence 'The Rescue Brigade'—a new departure which I hope readers feel has paid off.

P.J.L.C.

In the Mist of Life

BRIAN ALDISS

I HAD no friends now, only enemies and business acquaintances. It was through a contact with one of the business acquaintances that I found myself in the city of Baldersham. Although I had not been in Baldersham for twenty years, I soon managed to negotiate my way through the main thoroughfares, in spite of all the changes, and was pleased to do so.

My appointment was with a genial man called Overway, who expressed interest in the stamps I had to offer, and placed a considerable order with me, including a commission for a mint block of the 1935 Silver Jubilee 2½d in the rare Prussian blue shade. Afterwards he invited me for a drink at a nearby bar.

We sat and talked of philately and of the terrible things happening in our country. I was cheerful. Yet gradually I sensed a change coming over Overway and fell silent. His talk died away. We sat there while people at other tables chattered, two men with nothing to communicate. He rose, smiling, and excused himself, saying he must return to work.

Overway had felt the spiritual death within me. As always, I became conscious of my personality, which I drag about like a damp and heavy overcoat—not a real part of me, yet inseparable from me. I rose and left the bar, walking in the sun and trying to banish the feeling of despair. I grinned and nodded at people who passed in the street, telling myself proudly that I still remembered what it was like to smile spontaneously.

Then I recognised where I was. I was in a rather seedy street, Manx Street—the name meant nothing to me. There would be a florist's round the next corner, then a small hotel. What was it called? The Park Hotel. Of course, the Park! Would I ever forget it? Well, I had forgotten it for twenty years, but now it came back in pristine detail.

Speeding my pace, I turned the corner and looked about.

It was a drab street, made impersonal by huge grey concrete buildings which had not been there twenty years ago. At the end of the street was a multi-storey car park. It had been built over a little green park with a mound, on which daffodils blew when last I stood there.

The florist's was still in existence. Before it came a chapel I did not recollect. The windows were boarded up and the building was used as a furniture repository. But the florist still sold flowers and fruit. I recalled a rather dark little place, with a door recessed between small double windows. Now there was a chrome front, smart but shoddy.

And beyond—no Park Hotel. Instead, a gentlemen's hairdresser. I looked farther down the street. No hotel. A bank, a couple of building society offices. I peered into the hairdresser's. To one side of the salon was a door with an unlit neon sign in the transom. It said: PARK HOTEL: BED AND BREAKFAST.

A sudden warm emotion rose up in me, almost choking me like a gush of arterial blood. I literally had to steady myself against the jamb. Pauline! Oh, my dear Pauline! My beloved Pauline!

Without thought, I pushed the door open and went up a carpeted stair. At the top, inserted on a landing too narrow for it, was a desk with a potted fern, a price tariff, and a plastic notice which said RING FOR ATTEN-TION. I rang.

When I—when we—had been here, this was a thriving little hotel, rather prosperous, surely rather chic. There had been no hairdressing salon; instead, an elegant entrance and a bar, and had we not dined rather well in a snug little dining-room, she and I? And oh, Pauline, it was the first time you had consented to come away with me. . . . I was then the happiest of men.

With the varying fortunes of the nation, and of Baldersham, it was hardly surprising the hotel had gone downhill and had had to sell out or let off its ground floor. Standing there, looking at the dusty fern and the red plastic top of the desk, I remembered an old story I had read about a man returning to his home town after a number of years, twenty or more. He had found everything unchanged, streets, shops, houses, just as they had always been. But the people . . . how they had altered! The man hardly recognised the people. They had shrunk and stooped and withered and grown grey. Those who had been hearty young men were red-faced fools with fat paunches, those who had been spry and alert hobbled along on sticks. The story had terrified me at the time.

Yet reality was different. I was little changed, I thought, as far as external appearances went, since last I had been in Baldersham. I walked brisk and upright still. True, I had a lined brow, but what of that? Nor did a few white hairs count for much. Released from my overcoat of despair, I could enjoy life with the same snap as ever. Still and all, twenty years was a long time, and the marks of those years lay heavier on Baldersham than on me. The streets might bear the same names, yet in essence they were different streets. And they looked smaller and dirtier. The human amenities had shrunk. Even the elegant Park had dwindled into a drab bed-and-breakfast establishment, where the service was as bad as might be expected.

A woman stuck her head round a distant door and called, 'Do you want a room, love?'

Until then, I had hardly given the matter thought. There was nothing I wanted that this woman had it in her power to give. Yet a foolish sense of convention would not allow me simply to turn away. 'Yes,' I said.

She was a thick-set woman with a pale face and greying hair, the sort of woman who finds her way to that sort of place.

She made me sign a register and then led me up another flight of stairs. She opened a door to a narrow room overlooking the street.

'It's a bit noisy, but it's the only single I've got, all right?'

'Thanks.'

She looked at me. I put my philatelist's suitcase on the bed and looked at her. I was in a daze.

'Are you all right?' she asked.

'I was remembering. I have stayed in this hotel once before. I suppose you weren't here then, twenty years ago?'

She laughed. 'Not likely.'

'Do you own the hotel?'

She hesitated, resenting my curiosity. 'My husband and me took it over fifteen years ago, all right?'

When she had gone, I sat down on the bed. Pauline and I had been beyond harm. 'Innocent' was the word, and innocent our close delights in this hotel, because we had complete trust in each other. How beautiful she was, with her long fair hair, and how much we had laughed, from pure high spirits. Yet we had come to-gether—I had faced that unpalatable truth long ago—by cheating other people. Both Pauline and I were already married to others. After the Park, both our marriages collapsed. Grief all round, grief which we had weathered with hardly a thought, being together. And then. . . .

Numbly, I registered the frugal appurtenances of the room.

It had once been a larger room. A wooden partition cut across it, breaking its original symmetry. No doubt the woman and her husband had converted a double into two singles, finding that paid better for her trade. The partition wall was painted cream. The other three walls had a flock wallpaper with a distinctive pattern of funereal urns and macaws on it; it was faded but must once have been elegant.

Then memory roused again and I recognised it. I vividly remembered lying in the bed with Pauline against me, looking at the wallpaper and making some joke about it. A pun on the word 'urn'? For the briefest moment in time, I was back with Pauline, back twenty years, and all was as it had been when we had loved and trusted each other.

I stood up and looked at the bed—an old-fashioned double bed, despite the single room. It could have been in this very bed, tumbled since by who knew how many faithless bodies, that she and I had lain, limbs together, lips together, and vowed that we would always adore one another.

I threw myself on it and wept as I had not done over all the intervening years.

The fit did not last long. In the middle of it, I remembered another detail, an incident long submerged in time. She and I were eating breakfast downstairs in the little dining-room when a man rose from another table with a newspaper under his arm and passed our table on his way out. As he did so, he nodded familiarly to Pauline.

'Who's that?' I asked.

'Just someone I know.'

'Who is he?'

'Oh, he lives in Baldersham. He runs a restaurant. Well, a night club.'

Later, I found that he was called Paul Nokes. He turned up some weeks afterwards, and became a 'friend' of ours while our marriages were collapsing. The three of us used to drink together in his club and have a lot of fun. At one time, he had in tow a girl I rather fancied, although I never spoke to her alone. Her name came back to me now. Amy someone. A slender girl with dark hair and a pleasant disposition.

Pauline and I never bothered to get married. We set up in a flat in a decent part of London, and for a couple of years our life and my business prospered. Then one day I came home early from a stamp auction and found Paul Nokes in bed with Pauline. Paul and Pauline. . . .

People are supposed to be too sophisticated in this age to worry about such things. But his continued hypocritical insistence on friendship with me, Pauline's continued insistence that we all remain friends, wore me down. I should have behaved in the old-fashioned way that my nature dictated, and hit him hard. Instead, I weakly gave in to their protestations of friendship all round. A year later, I discovered that she was still secretly meeting him.

Although they again protested love for me—yes, both of them—I felt myself utterly betrayed. My own sins merely added an element of self-betrayal. I stood it for a week. Then I packed a suitcase and left the flat. After which, I never saw either Pauline or Paul Nokes again.

His empty laughing face, his unfathomable eyes, rose before me.

The woman went slowly downstairs. She paused on the landing. She looked at the register and then shuffled along to her private room.

An electric fire burned there. A man sat over it, reading a newspaper.

'Customer?' he asked, without looking up from the sports page.

'A feller called Robert Gore. Doesn't look at all well to me.'

'Where did you put him?'

'Over here. No. 5. I'm just going down the street to do a bit of shopping, all right?'

'I may pop over to the Fox later, if you aren't back. What did you say his name was?'

'Robert Gore.'

'I used to have a pal called Bob Gore, ages ago. Amy?'

'What? Answer the bell while I'm out, won't you?'

'Don't forget to go to the bank.'

She lit a cigarette as she turned to the door and said with some affection, 'Paul, you're the laziest layabout I ever met up with. *Or* put up with.'

He glanced up from the newsprint and grinned. 'What do you expect me to do? Take up Yoga?'

When she had left, he turned comfortably back to his paper. A noise soon distracted him and he looked towards the ceiling. A sound like crying from No. 5.

He sat for some while, gnawing his thumbnail. Then he stood up and put his feet into slippers.

Bob Gore? It couldn't be. Not after sixteen or more years.

After some hesitation, he moved to the door. The crying stopped. Curiosity impelled him into the passage.

A few random recollections came to him. Bob Gore—and some bird he used to shack up with. A blonde. Her name had vanished in the mists of time.

He went quietly up the stairs, grinning broadly to himself. The years went by but there had been some fun in the old days, all good friends around. It would be a laugh to meet a real old mate again. If it was the same Bob Gore.

He tapped on the door of No. 5 and entered, smiling.

Surface Textures

ANITA DESAI

IT WAS all her own fault, she later knew—but how could she have helped it? When she stood, puckering her lips, before the fruit barrow in the market and, after sullen consideration, at last plucked a rather small but nicely ripened melon out of a heap on display, her only thought had been: Is it worth a rupee and fifty paise? The lichees looked more poetic, in large clusters like some prickly grape of a charming rose colour, their long stalks and stiff grey leaves tied in a bunch above them—but were expensive. Mangoes were what the children were eagerly waiting for—the boys, she knew, were raiding the mango trees in the school compound daily and their stomach-aches were a result, she told them, of the unripe mangoes they ate and for which they carried paper packets of salt to school in their pockets instead of handkerchiefs; but, leave alone the expense, the ones the fruiterer held up to her enticingly were bound to be sharp and sour for all their parakeet shades of rose and saffron: it was still too early for mangoes. So she put the melon in her string bag, rather angrily, paid the man his one rupee and fifty paise, which altered his expression from one of promise and enticement to one of disappointment and contempt, and trailed off towards the vegetable barrow.

That, she later saw, was the beginning of it all, for if

the melon seemed puny to her and boring to the children, from the start her husband regarded it with eyes that seemed newly opened. One would have thought he had never seen a melon before. All through the meal his eyes remained fixed on the plate in the centre of the table with its big button of a yellow melon. He left most of his rice and pulses on his plate, to her indignation. While she scolded, he reached out to touch the melon that so captivated him. With one finger he stroked the coarse grain of its rind, rough with the upraised crisscross of pale veins. Then he ran his fingers up and down the green streaks that divided it into even quarters as by green silk threads, so tenderly. She was clearing away the plates and did not notice till she came back from the kitchen.

'Aren't you going to cut it for us?' she asked, pushing the knife across to him.

He gave her a reproachful look as he picked up the knife and went about dividing the melon into quarter-moon portions with sighs that showed how it pained him.

'Come on, come on,' she said, roughly, 'the boys have to get back to school.'

He handed them their portions and watched them scoop out the icy orange flesh with a fearful expression on his face—as though he were observing cannibals at a feast. She had not the time to pay any attention to it then, but later described it as horror. And he did not eat his own slice. When the boys rushed away, he bowed his head over his plate and regarded it.

'Are you going to fall asleep?' she cried, a little frightened.

'Oh no,' he said, in that low mumble that always exasperated her—it seemed a sign to her of evasiveness and pusillanimity, this mumble—'oh no, no.' Yet he did not object when she seized the plate and carried it off to the kitchen—merely picked up the knife that was left behind and, picking a flat melon-seed off its edge where it had remained stuck, held it between two fingers, fondling it delicately. Continuing to do this, he left the house.

The melon might have been the apple of knowledge for Harish—so deadly its poison that he did not even need to bite into it to imbibe it: that long, devoted look had been enough. As he walked back to his office, which issued ration cards to the population of their town, he looked about him vaguely but with hunger, his eyes resting not on the things on which people's eyes normally rest—signboards, the traffic, the number of an approaching bus—but on such things, normally considered nondescript and unimportant, as the paving-stones on which their feet momentarily pressed, the length of wire in a railing at the side of the road, a pattern of grime on the window-pane of a disused printing-press. . . . Amongst such things his eyes roved and hunted and, when he was seated at his desk in the office, his eyes continued to slide about—that was Sheila's phrase later: 'slide about'—in a musing, calculating way, over the surface of the crowded desk, about the corners of the room, even across the ceiling. He seemed unable to focus them on a file or a card long enough to put his signature to them; they lay unsigned and the people in the queue outside went for another day without rice and sugar and kerosene for their lamps and Janta cookers. Harish searched—slid about, hunted, gazed—and at last found sufficiently interesting a thick book of rules that lay beneath a stack of files. Then his hand reached out—not to pull the book to him or open it, but to run the ball of his thumb across the edges of the pages. In their large number and irregular cut, so closely laid out like some crisp palimpsest, his eyes seemed to find something of riveting interest and his thumb of tactile wonder. All afternoon he massaged the cut edges of the book's 700-odd pages—tenderly, won-deringly. All afternoon his eyes gazed upon them with strange devotion. At five o'clock, punctually, the office shut and the queue disintegrated into vociferous grum-bles and threats as people went home instead of to the ration shops, empty-handed instead of loaded with those necessary but, to Harish, so dull comestibles.

Although Government service is as hard to depart from as to enter—so many letters to be written, forms to be filled, files to be circulated, petitions to be made that it hardly seems worthwhile—Harish was, after some time, dismissed: time he happily spent judging the difference between white blotting-paper and pink (pink is flatter, denser, white spongier) and the texture of blotting-paper stained with ink and that which is fresh, that which has been put to melt in a saucer of cold tea and that which has been doused in a pot of ink. Harish was dismissed.

The first few days Sheila stormed and screamed like some shrill, wet hurricane about the house. 'How am I to go to market and buy vegetables for dinner? I don't even have enough for that. What am I to feed the boys tonight? No more milk for them. The washerwoman is asking for her bill to be paid. Do you hear? Do you *hear*? And we shall have to leave this flat. Where shall we go?' He listened—or didn't—sitting on a cushion before her mirror, fingering the small silver box in which she kept the red *kum-kum* that daily cut a gash from one end of her scalp to the other after her toilet. It was of dark, almost blackened silver, with a whole forest embossed on it—banana groves, elephants, peacocks and jackals. He rubbed his thumb over its cold, raised surface.

After that, she wept. She lay on her bed in a bath of tears and perspiration, and it was only because of the kindness of their neighbours that they did not starve to death the very first week, for even those who most disliked and distrusted Harish—'Always said he looks like a hungry hyena,' said Mr Bhatia who lived below their flat, 'not human at all, but like a hungry, hunchbacked hyena hunting along the road'—felt for the distraught wife and the hungry children (who did not really mind as long as there were sour green mangoes to steal and devour) and looked to them. Such delicacies as Harish's family had never known before arrived in stainless-steel and brass dishes, with delicate unobstrusiveness. For a while wife and children gorged on sweetmeats made with fresh buffalo milk, on pulses cooked according to grandmother's recipes, on stuffed bread and the first pomegranates of the season. But, although delicious, these offerings came in small quantities and irregularly, and soon they were really starving.

'I suppose you want me to take the boys home to my parents,' said Sheila bitterly, getting up from the bed.

'Any other man would regard that as the worst disgrace of all—but not you. What is my shame to you? I will have to hang my head and crawl home and beg my father to look after us, since you won't,' and that was what she did. He was sorry, very sorry, to see her pack the little silver *kum-kum* box in her black trunk and carry it away.

Soon afterwards, officials of the Ministry of Works, Housing and Land Development came and turned Harish out, cleaned and painted the flat and let in the new tenants, who could hardly believe their luck—they had been told so often they couldn't expect a flat in that locality for at least another two years.

The neighbours lost sight of Harish. Once some children reported they had seen him lying under the *pipal* tree at the corner of their school compound, staring fixedly at the red gashes cut into the papery bark and, later, a boy who commuted to school on a suburban train claimed to have seen him on the railway platform, sitting against a railing like some tattered beggar, staring across the criss-cross of shining rails. But, next day, when the boy got off the train, he did not see Harish again.

Harish had gone hunting. His slow, silent walk gave him the appearance of sliding rather than walking over the surface of the roads and fields, rather like a snail except that his movement was not as smooth as a snail's, but stumbling, as if he had only recently become one and was still unused to the pace. Not only his eyes and his hands but even his bare feet seemed to be feeling the earth carefully, in search of an interesting surface. Once he found it, he would pause, his whole body would gently collapse across it, and hours—perhaps days—would be devoted to its investigation and worship. Outside the town the land was rocky and bare, and this was Harish's especial paradise, each rock having a surface of such exquisite roughness, of such perfection in shape and design, as to keep him occupied and ecstatic for weeks together. Then the river beyond the rock quarries drew him away, and there he discovered the joy of fingering silk-smooth stalks and reeds, stems and leaves.

Shepherd children, seeing him stumble about the reeds, plunging thigh-deep into the water in order to pull out a water-lily with its cool, sinuous stem, fled screaming, not certain whether this was a man or a hairy water-snake. Their mothers came, some with stones and some with canes at the ready, but when they saw Harish, his skin parched to a violet shade, sitting on the bank and gazing at the transparent stem of the lotus, they fell back, crying, 'Wah!' gathered closer together, advanced, dropped their canes and stones, held their children still by their hair and shoulders, and came to bow to him. Then they hurried back to the village, chattering. They had never had a Swami to themselves in these arid parts. Nor had they seen a Swami who looked holier, more inhuman than Harish with his matted hair, his blue, starved skin and single-focused eyes. So, in the evening, one brought him a brass vessel of milk, another a little rice. They pushed their children before them and made them drop flowers at his feet. When Harish stooped and felt among the offerings for something his fingers could respond to, they were pleased, they felt accepted. 'Swami-ji,' they whispered, 'speak.'

Harish did not speak, and his silence made him still

holier, safer. So they worshipped him, fed and watched over him, interpreting his moves in their own fashion, and Harish, in turn, watched over their offerings and worshipped.

Space Fiction

GEOFFREY HOUSEHOLD

PEPE DE CEA must have remembered that I was born in Argentina and could communicate with Spanish-speaking horses. I was also the only one of his intimate friends likely to be at home and in bed at 1.30 a.m. He did not even apologise for his arrival.

'It's my mother-in-law again,' he explained. 'And I will not calm myself. And I do not need a drink. Get dressed and come!'

'Oh, God! Not donkeys?'

'A mule. When I came home it was in the courtyard.'

Mrs Fellowes had a vague and gossamer charm. Her daughter, Barbara, who had impulsively married Pepe when he was a minor attaché in the London embassy, inherited the charm and added the assurance proper to a young Spanish matron. Pepe adored the pair of them and welcomed the frequent visits of his mother-in-law to Madrid, although on occasion he had to explain her peculiarities to the police. Nothing could shake Mrs Fellowes' belief that Spaniards were cruel to animals. She had a habit of wandering about the more primitive quarters of the city—since animals had pretty well disappeared from the glittering centre—with a bag of carrots and breathless rebukes.

'She hasn't stolen it?' I asked.

'She says it chased her home trying to bite her.'

'What is she doing about it?'

'Nothing. It terrified her. She has gone to bed, more convinced than ever that my cruel countrymen brutalise their animals with whips and red-hot pokers.'

'And Barbara?'

'Barbara is with her. In the way of women they have both decided it is all my fault.'

'I don't see how it could be. You were out.'

'That's why.'

'Well, shoo the mule away!'

'I can't. You never saw such a vicious-looking brute. I think its mother was a hyena. Its ears are about half a metre long and it bares its teeth at me.'

'Any flame from its nostrils?'

'Not yet. But don't light a match when it snorts at you!'

I had no experience of mules, only knowing that some of them can kick forwards, which a horse usually can't, and that the seat of one's pants is by no means safe even when holding the head. Still, it seemed a simple matter to accompany an unduly nervous friend and remove the beast. Other complications he would have to settle himself. The mule's proprietor might turn out to be an angrily obstinate carter who would refuse compensation and insist on an official complaint. The worst risk was what Mrs Fellowes would say in court if the police ran her in. No magistrate was going to take a lenient view after being lectured on his compatriots' supposed cruelty to animals.

Pepe's seventeenth-century house was in an unfashionable district off the Atocha, but within its courtyard he had the quiet and privacy of a village. He parked his flashy sports car in the street and we entered the court through a narrow archway. The mule was standing on the cobbles—a huge, black draught mule, a mediaeval gargoyle of a mule. Half a wooden post dangled from its halter. Its tail was bald except for an obscene tuft at the end. Its snarling teeth were bright yellow in the light over the front door, and quite long enough for any reasonable hyena.

'It pulled that post down for the sake of carrots?' I asked.

'Or to attack my mother-in-law. When they met, it was tied up in front of a tavern with the cart alongside.'

'Well, we'd better start with some more carrots.'

Edging past the mule, Pepe disappeared into the house. He returned with only two carrots, saying that he couldn't find any more in the larder. I sent him back to forage for something else and to assure his women, if they came down, that I would handle the problem without unnecessary violence. I certainly was not going to force that mule to do anything against its wishes.

I advanced upon it, preceded by the longer carrot. One ear was reassuringly forward; the other was halfway down its neck, apparently investigating sounds from the broken post. It accepted the carrot with a snort and a start as if it had been dreaming of the things and suddenly found they were a real presence.

With head and neck aligned like a striking snake, and baring its fearful yellow teeth, it proceeded to examine me. I stood still only because I did not dare to turn my back. Its oddly prehensile nose was velvet and friendly. Its brown eyes, though mischievous, were showing no white. When I found that it enjoyed being patted and talked to, I realised that the fighting-stallion effect was artificial. That mule had been deliberately taught to smile—either to keep off thieves or, more probably, to earn free drinks for its owner. Quite obviously it had been treated with affection as one of the family. But the family was poor. Carrots had seldom come its way. Its intent in breaking loose and chasing Mrs Fellowes into a smart trot had been to get some more from her bag.

Pepe, returning from the house with a long parcel in greaseproof paper, was impressed. If he had been brought up among horses he would soon have seen, as I did, that this hideous monstrosity was as friendly as a child's pony. But I did not disturb his opinion of me and asked him what he had in the parcel.

'Brazos de Gitana,' he replied. 'It was all I could find. Barbara is giving a party tomorrow. Do you think he'll like it?'

I said it would certainly be new to him. There were over a couple of feet of this delectable cake, somewhat resembling a Swiss roll and stuffed with gently foaming cream. I tried a piece on the mule. I doubt if he found it as welcome as carrots, but it was an agreeable change from hay and the remains of the family's chickpeas. He faced it boldly and with growing interest like a man trying out a first-class French restaurant with a luncheon voucher.

'Do you think you can entice him back with that?' Pepe asked.

'I think *we* can. Where to?'

'She isn't quite sure. You know how she wanders about dreaming that she is St Francis. She believes the tavern was somewhere between the Atocha station and the Plaza de la Cebada.'

They were the best part of a mile from each other. We were bound to attract a following of idle and interested spectators while leading a draught mule on a random search through the back streets of Madrid. Pepe could not be anything but a young and moneyed *señorito* and I am always recognised as English.

'Have you decided what we are going to say to the police?' I asked him, removing the length of worm-eaten post from the mule's halter. It was deeply carved and suggested the pillar of a veranda rather than a mere hitching-post.

'We just found it wandering. And you with British public spirit and responsibility. . . .'

'On the contrary. You, Pepe, with the splendid and generous impulse of a Spaniard. . . .'

'Suppose you ride it?' he suggested.

I pointed out that there was no reason to believe the mule had ever been ridden and that it was a long way to the ground. If we had a cart, we might drive it.

The mention of wheels brought Pepe back to the automobile age.

'I'll run down to the Atocha goods yard and hire a cattle-truck,' he said. 'There's sure to be one about and we'll only need it for ten minutes.'

That was probable. The tavern and deserted cart could not be far away, since the mule seemed to have vanished

round corners and into Pepe's courtyard before anyone
could spot what had happened and take off after it.

When he had left, the night wore on for me and my
peaceable companion. In the street outside there was
even an hour of silence. I supplied the mule with a
bucket of water and another mouthful of cream and
sponge cake. He then went to sleep on his feet; so did I
on the front steps, for I felt reluctant to ring the bell
and wake up the house just to tell Barbara and Mrs
Fellowes that their mule at present was contented and
affectionate. While the future was uncertain, witnesses
were better away.

About four in the morning Pepe silently freewheeled
into the courtyard, taking the corner with the skill of
long practice.

'Got one!' he exclaimed. 'There was nothing at the
station, so I had to go down to the slaughterhouse. I
found a man who had just delivered some cattle and was
glad to have the job.'

'Did you tell him what it was?'

'Only to move a beast to the Atocha station.'

A dilapidated van backed up to the archway, which
was too low for it to enter the court. The driver came
round and let down the tailboard to form a ramp. He was
a real sun-dried tough from Burgos. He said that if he
had expected a mule, which he hadn't, it should not be
one frothing at the mouth. God knows what he did
expect! Livestock in the centre of Madrid must be rare.

I had no time to explain that the froth was whipped
cream, for the mule panicked. Evidently it had never
travelled in a van. It folded its ears back and flung up its

gaunt, black head to have a better look, wrenching the halter from my hand. The man from Burgos circled cautiously round it and caught it a whack with his stick which would have earned him a lecture from Mrs Fellowes. The mule, too, was scandalised by this normal method of starting nervous cattle up a ramp. It bucked and let go with its off hind. Not viciously. It was only protesting against such treatment when out of harness. That hoof fairly whistled past the driver's stomach; the head then twisted right round at an unnatural angle to inspect him.

I entered the van with the sticky parcel of Brazos de Gitana. That was effective. The mule bared its yellow fangs in the usual smile and clattered up the ramp at me. I tied it up while it lovingly filled my ear with cream. The driver had taken refuge in his cab; so I closed up the tailboard and joined Pepe in the front seat.

The driver was crossing himself. I think it may have occurred to him that we had just exorcised the old house and that this grinning weremule was the result. He was in a nightmare anyway. Nothing made sense. When Pepe directed him to the station and then, as soon as we were safely away from home, turned him off to the Cebada through a labyrinth of one-way streets, he shrugged his shoulders and gave it up.

It did not take us long to discover the mule's starting point: a little square with a patch of paving in the middle on which were some empty carts. Outside a tavern was a narrow veranda with a sagging roof. One of its supporting columns was broken. An old-fashioned carter was being supported by the tavern-keeper and his fellows while two policemen tried to take notes of his remarks. He was magnificently in liquor. So, I think, were the rest of them. If they had only recently noticed the absence of the mule, it stood to reason.

Fortunately we were loitering along the opposite side of the square, too far away for the driver to hear what all the excitement was about. Pepe snapped at him to turn right and so startled the man that he did. We bounced the wrong way up a one-way street, straightened ourselves out and were compelled to arrive at the Puerta del Sol.

'And now?' the driver asked, pulling up right in the centre of Madrid.

'Straight on,' said Pepe confidently.

There was really no straight on; but the man from Burgos took it that he should continue north—which he did, looking more and more suspicious, until there was little of Madrid left. We could not discuss in his presence what on earth we were to do. We did not dare to tip the mule out into the road in front of a witness who knew Pepe's address and was certain to talk.

'To whom does this animal belong?' the driver asked sullenly.

'Friend, it belongs to us both,' Pepe answered.

'Then listen, both of you! I am not a man for jokes. The transport of cattle is my living. There are inspections. There are licences. What we are going to do is to stop at the nearest police station.'

I foresaw no trouble in clearing myself of the charge of stealing a mule; but Spanish summary justice is slow, and it would be at least a month before my passport was returned and I was formally congratulated on my innocence. As for Pepe, he could only denounce his mother-in-law's habits and opinions—which would not lead to peace at home—or pay an immense fine as a gilded youth who had amused himself at the expense of the public.

The mention of licences worked on his despairing imagination. He said: 'As you like. It's not our fault that the chap we expected never turned up. To us the police can do nothing.'

'Nor to me.'

'If God wills. I don't know the regulations of the veterinary service.'

'What have the vets to do with it?'

'*Hombre!* You don't think I would get rid of a family pet for no reason?'

'Family pet, my foot!'

'You cannot imagine how fond of it my father was,' Pepe protested, looking hurt. 'And now it has to be put down.'

'What's the matter with it?'

'Well, you saw how it attacked with open mouth this gentleman whom it has known since it was a foal. In all fairness I must advise you to disinfect your van.'

'Jesus! I have children at home!'

'There's nothing to worry about. It hasn't bitten you. You have only to keep your trap shut.'

'I'm not going another step,' said the driver, stopping abruptly in a melancholy nowhere intensified by the first grey of dawn.

'But I could not know you had children. Then we have

only to settle accounts. We have come six times the distance you expected, so I'll make it six times the price. Agreed?'

'Since I am on my way home anyway, I won't say no. But for the sake of us all, not a word!' the driver added anxiously. 'If this came out, they could order my van to be burned.'

Pepe gave him his solemn promise to keep quiet and we both had the effrontery to shake his hand.

There was no time to waste. The streets would soon be stirring. We stopped and unloaded in the first private spot we could see: a blind alley between a wall and the blank side of a narrow, isolated tenement house. I felt it a low trick to abandon this accomplished animal so far from home, but the police would soon identify it and meanwhile there was plenty of garbage for its entertainment. When the driver had reversed into the cover of the alley, the mule clattered down upon the concrete, ears forward and delighted to see me again. As soon as I had replaced the tailboard, the van gave one leap towards Burgos and disappeared.

Leaving the mule with one ear exploring the silence and the other twitching above a rubbish bin, Pepe and I tiptoed away. We had just turned the corner into the street when we heard it walking after us. I think it was not the first time the mule had been lost, and it had learned from experience—for all the horse species are nervous creatures and remember panic—that when on its own it became an outlaw hateful to human beings instead of a hard-working family friend. Pepe and I represented not only Brazos de Gitana but security.

The only escape route was through the front door of the tenement house and up the first flight of concrete steps. The mule stood outside extending its monstrous ears in our direction like the antennae of a visiting Martian. It would have heard nothing but the vague noises of early workers about to tumble out of bed if Pepe had not nervously started up another flight.

His footsteps were enough. The mule tripped quietly and confidently up the stairs and arrived on the landing with every sign of lasting affection and its nose in my pocket looking for crumbs. Finding no more sponge cake it started off after Pepe in the hope that he might have a bit left.

Pepe still did not understand those bared teeth. He dashed upstairs, making far more noise than the careful mule, which must have been bred from a mountain pack-donkey. When all three of us were at last reunited we found we were on the fifth and last landing. The flats below were stirring but without excitement. A door shut. Two men exchanged good-mornings. The day's work had started.

The mule remained as still as we. If my theory is correct, he had caught the smell of our anxiety and assumed that we too were hiding from the public hostility which descended on him whenever his master, who should never have taught him to smile, spent long and forgetful hours in Madrid taverns.

When all was comparatively quiet again and later risers had pulled the blankets over their ears, I tried to persuade the mule to accompany me downstairs and into the open. He didn't like it. He wouldn't have it. The treads were narrow and a hoof slipped. He backed cautiously on to the landing again.

'That's fixed him,' Pepe said. 'Now all we have to do is to run.'

I refused to risk damaging a valuable animal which had put its mistaken trust in his mother-in-law. If deserted it might impulsively decide to follow at any cost and break a leg or its neck or probably both. I reminded Pepe that we had set out with the intention of returning stolen goods.

'But we can't just stay here!' he screamed in a whisper.

There was something in that. Front doors might open at any minute. A sense of humour was too much to expect so early in the morning. We should be shouted down by all the inhabitants of the building and, as news of the mule spread, by those of the neighbouring tenement houses as well.

On this top floor were two apartments, one occupied and one still to let. Between them a half-flight of steps continued up to a little penthouse in which was a wooden door giving access to the flat roof and the washing-lines. I suggested that we should go up and see if there was anywhere to hide.

'Suppose the mule comes too?'

Any fool could see it was impossible, I replied. The door was smaller than a standard door and manifestly too low for the mule to pass through.

But he could and he did tackle the steps. It was amazing how that great Satanic black brute could tread so daintily. Approaching from below, at an angle of forty-five degrees to the horizontal, his head and neck of course went through the door easily, and before we could shut it. He liked what he saw and he liked us. He stretched out his forelegs alongside his neck and gave a heave with his hind. The door-frame shuddered in its plaster, and he was through. He was on the roof.

It was near sunrise. We could see the range of the Guadarrama and the distant, fortunate traffic on the road to Burgos. I hoped the mule would be patient and enjoy the view, but it was thirsty and, smelling water, it reared up with no more trouble than a black cat, forelegs upon the roof tank, prodigiously outlined against the dawn. We crept away and bolted the door behind us after removing a few tell-tale black hairs from the lintel.

We were just about to sneak down the stairs to liberty and were discussing in whispers whether we could get away with a story of having come up to visit a girl or whether no story at all would be necessary. With luck it wouldn't be; there was still no one about. And then a vast, muffled crash, without splinterings, crackings or any preliminaries, shook the top storey of that house in a single tremor.

'God help us, he's gone through the roof!' Pepe exclaimed.

We waited. Nothing happened. It was the occupied flat into which the mule had fallen, but there was no protest from the tenant. Beneath us were only some faintly audible expletives from lower flats. The inhabitants were probably accustomed to any sort of thud echoing through the whole of that cheap, shockingly built tenement house. This one could have been caused by a wardrobe collapsing, or father falling off a ladder and tearing the sink out by the roots.

But one could bet that such a thump would alarm the owner if he lived on his own palsied premises. Far down the bare well of the staircase someone burst out of a flat, hammered on the opposite door and routed out a tenant who, at a guess, acted as part-time porter. Both of them started up the stairs, loudly debating about what could have tumbled down and giving us time to take refuge in a cupboard under the half-flight of steps, crouched among mops and buckets. The pair unbolted the roof door and saw at a glance that everything was standing up which should have been. The side of the penthouse concealed the hole through which the mule had vanished, and naturally they were not looking for a hole since there was nothing which could have made one.

We remained where we were, panic-stricken through long minutes.

'The empty flat!' Pepe suggested at last. 'If we drop off the parapet, we'll land on the balcony.'

That was true enough, provided we did not go through it; so we tiptoed back to the roof, the landlord having left the door on the latch, but then were so flustered that we could not decide which balcony was the right one. In order to get our bearings we opened the door for a moment and looked down. It was like opening up a wasps' nest. At least six women were screaming at each other simultaneously.

The balcony of the empty flat held, though quivering as we hit it. The concrete balustrade was high enough to hide us if we squatted down, and there we had to stay. The window which led into the flat was shuttered and locked.

I insisted that I was only an interested foreigner, that I would have nothing to do with forcible entry and that probably someone would come to inspect the flat during the day and let us out. Pepe replied that we might just as well add burglary to our other crimes and that what bothered him even more than his diplomatic career was Barbara. If he didn't get home soon, she would assume he had been killed by her mother's mule and telephone the police.

He sat down by the shutter and began to cut away the lower slats with a pocket-knife. It was a long job; the builder's carpenter had been more conscientious than his masons. Meanwhile a small crowd gathered in the street, all talking at once, while women fluttered off to spread the news to other tenements. A self-important fellow on the balcony immediately below us was conducting a conversation with two other balconies and the street.

'What's happening?' Pepe asked me, struggling to loosen slats without doing violent and audible damage.

'A lady in hysterics and a dressing-gown is saying that she is a respectable woman and that her bed has hitherto remained inviolate. I suspect she was in somebody else's.'

'I am not interested in local scandal.'

'Yes, you are. She says that when she returned to her flat from an errand of mercy she found a mule in her bed. It was sleeping like a Christian with its head on her pillow. She thought it was the Devil.'

'Her theology seems a bit muddled.'

'Well, one can see what she meant.'

'Have they sent for the police?'

'They have—and the fire brigade.'

'How do they think it got there?'

'The chap underneath is talking about a rain of frogs in his grandfather's day.'

'A café talker! Irrelevant as always!'

'No, he isn't. It's agreed all round that the mule dropped from the sky. Even if it could climb stairs, it could not get through the door. And the landlord swears that anyway the door was bolted.'

'Why the hell wasn't it hurt?' Pepe asked, wrenching free another couple of slats.

I listened until I got the public verdict. The sturdy common sense of the people had arrived at the only possible answer. The mule had come down on a parachute. On the other hand no parachute had been found. The persistent and dogmatic voice on the balcony below said that parachutes were now superseded, that his wife's cousin had told him that the Americans were experimenting with anti-gravity.

'Like monkeys,' someone answered obscurely.

'It is the Russians who use monkeys. From the Americans one can expect nothing less than a mule.'

Pepe was inclined to be anti-American, so I passed this on to him as evidence of their unassailable prestige. At the time it did not seem to register. He lay on his back and kicked the glass out of the pane behind the slats he had removed.

'Crawl through that quick!' he ordered. 'And mind broken glass!'

We padded through two empty rooms and opened the front door a crack. Not a face was turned in our direction. The passage and living-room of the opposite flat were full of tenants, whispering to each other and trying to get a glimpse of the mule. It must have been still luxuriating on the squashed bed, weary of travel and possibly smiling in its sleep. Evidently no one had the courage to wake it up.

Silently shutting the door of the flat behind us, we mingled with the overflow and started to peer over shoulders. That was a mistake. The owner of the house spotted at once that we had no right to be there. It had not occurred to us that downstairs a policeman had already been posted to keep out the curious.

'And where have you come from?' he demanded suspiciously.

'Would you be good enough to tell me where I can find the proprietor of this building?' Pepe asked.

'I am.'

Alongside the landlord was a young Spanish clerk, black-suited, trying to look experienced in such accidents.

'And this gentleman?'

'The local agent of my insurance company.'

'Then it could not be more convenient,' Pepe said with the impressive, formal courtesy of the diplomatic service. 'I am the official interpreter of the American Embassy. This is the Technical Officer. He speaks, unfortunately, little Spanish. Now, where can we talk freely?'

I was alarmed that Pepe should have deprived me of any control over whatever he was planning. However, the landlord's shabby ground-floor flat to which he led us at least contained a much-needed drink. Since we were in the respectable company of capital and insurance, the policeman in the hall ignored us.

'As between allies we beg for the utmost discretion,' Pepe began. 'Now, we understand that in the course of an experiment in the stratosphere some animal was prematurely released. . . .'

I got it at last, and interrupted in English: 'Ask him which animal!'

Pepe did so.

'Ah, only the mule!' he exclaimed in a tone of relief. 'The mule, yes! It was computerised for 41.63 North, 19.00 West. A cruiser is standing by.'

'Where is that?' the insurance agent asked.

'North of the Azores. In the circumstances an unacceptable error.'

'But my roof!' the landlord complained. 'One does not expect such carelessness from a great and honourable nation.'

'That is the reason for our visit. If you and your agent will be good enough to call at the American Embassy at 11.30 precisely and ask for the Naval Attaché, the matter will be settled on the spot. All we require, as I said, is the utmost discretion.'

'And what shall we do with the mule?'

'To avoid questions and to give an appearance of normality the Minister of the Interior has suggested that the fire brigade should winch it down and hand it over to the police.'

I got up and shook hands all round.

'Your car is waiting?' the landlord asked.

'We do not leave a car in public places where it might

arouse embarrassing curiosity,' Pepe replied.

Two streets away we found a bus and were home for breakfast. The next day's papers informed us without comment that a mule, inexplicably discovered on an isolated roof, had been tranquillised and removed by the fire brigade and eventually restored to its owner. The incident did not even make the front page. Of course not. Only the improbable is news. The impossible is not.

But I could not leave it at that. I spent several evenings haunting the Plaza de la Cebada until I came face to face with that unmistakable animal, outside the same tavern and now between the shafts of a cart. Its proud possessor told me over his second litre that, by God, I was a friend and so he did not wish me to put my faith in rumours. It was quite untrue, he said, that his mule had strayed into the garden of the American Embassy and been launched into space, travelling twice round the world between midnight and dawn. No, not at all! For the sake of its smile and numerous accomplishments it had without doubt been stolen by a circus manager and escaped from the van—unhappy, loyal creature—into the nearest house.

And then a woman! Always a woman behind every commotion, true? Her husband was away, so she left the door open for her lover. And in walked Sebastiano.

The carter rose from the table, steadying himself with a hand upon my shoulder, unharnessed the mule and ordered: 'Aupa, Sebastiano!'

The mule obediently performed a courbette and pawed the air as if trained in the Spanish Riding School. I could at last understand its apocalyptic pose against the water-tank.

'So you see,' the carter went on, 'she fled in panic, slamming the door, and my clever Sebastiano tried to cut his way out through the ceiling. That was enough to bring the roof down. Now it can be seen how they build houses for the poor!'

The police, I gathered, had tended to approve his theory though it was hardly more believable than Pepe's impromptu space fiction. I sympathised with them. Anyone possessed by Sebastiano was bound instinctively to be in favour of ascent from a hell rather than descent from heaven.

The Consolations of Religion

PETER KEMP

ON THE FIRST DAY of the last term, Deirdre Blain made sure she arrived early. Shattering the six-week silence of the corridors with her spasmodic cough and noisy steps, she hurried to the staff-room, almost running up the stairs; paused outside the dark grain-varnished door; suddenly thrust it open; and then briefly smiled on finding the room, as she had hoped, still unoccupied.

Outside, around the school, and very audibly, that morning's rain was beating into puddles from the day before. And inside the building, too, it was cold for early autumn, damp and raw: so that the first thing Deirdre did was to stoop and light the fire, a large old-fashioned gas appliance in a black iron casing. As flames reddened its chalky mantles, she coughed and turned away. Shaking the wet from her drenched coat, she half-flung, half-hung it on the rack and rapidly crossed to the room's one mirror. Here, she rubbed her face dry with a handkerchief; then began to comb her hair, normally a reddish colour but now darker from the rain. Blackened and straightened in this way, it contrasted sharply with the pallor and irregularity of the face it framed—a bony sallow structure whose features were less noticeable than the marks around them.

Deirdre's pale eyes, though sharp, were narrow, and

the brows above them sparse. Her nose was a thin and rather brittle-looking ridge. Her lips were meagre, too: just a sufficient border to seal up the skin around the cranny of her mouth. But where endowment had left blanks, experience had written. Over the somewhat extensive areas of skin stretching between her face's little features there now spread a spidery commentary of dissatisfaction-lines. It was a message Deirdre had not attempted to conceal. She wore no make-up—though her eyes were shadowed, almost fashionably, by insomnia-smudges and, plastered high across one jutting cheek, there was, like an old beauty-patch, a quite sizeable mole.

Impatiently tugging a plastic comb through her wet hair, Deirdre surveyed all this in the oblong glass, her expression relaxing into a contemptuous despondency. Then, like limp tissue touched by acid, her face tautened with sarcasm. As often happened when she looked at herself in a mirror, she was remembering what Aunt Edith used to say whenever she caught her doing this. 'Yes, miss'—Deirdre could still hear the vehement hiss of those convinced and self-approving tones—'yes, you stare into that thing long enough and you know who you'll be seeing, don't you? You'll be seeing the Devil, that's who.' Aunt Edith had spent quite a lot of time elaborating bleakly on this theme. Vanity had seemed to obsess her. It was the worst of sins, she was given to claiming, since it had brought about the downfall of Lucifer. Nearer home, Deirdre had gradually discovered, it had also brought about the downfall of her own mother, de- plorable unmarried Gertrude who had taken in her late teens to make-up and mortal sins. One of the latter—committed with a local policeman, according to Aunt Edith—had led to the advent of Deirdre. The policeman was transferred to another district. Quite soon after the birth, Gertrude left for Liverpool. A picture postcard of the Calgary Stampede, giving no further indication as to her whereabouts, arrived with slightly mis-spelled greetings six Christmases later. Apart from this, Deirdre had had no contact with her mother for the forty-one years of her life. Instead, as a child, she had been more or less adopted by Aunt Edith, who was as different from Gertrude as holy water—of which she kept a stoup in every room—was from bargain-basement perfume. Tightening her lips and doing her duty, Aunt Edith had brought Deirdre up and warned her against vanity. Well, thought Deirdre, smiling an irritable smile as she put away her comb, Aunt Edith needn't have worried. When she looked into a mirror, then as now, plainness stared her in the face. It had chaperoned her through what Aunt Edith called 'the flighty years'—just like the guardian angel keeping demons at bay in her aunt's favourite holy picture, the one that marked the place of the Communion Prayers in her missal, *The Garden of the Soul.* And now she was respectably married to a good Catholic husband, and their daughter was legitimate and baptised and confirmed.

Making a detour to collect an ashtray—it was a souvenir of Fatima—on her way back across to the fire, Deirdre settled in an armchair, stretched her wet shoes towards the hissing heat, and waited with a cigarette. Eight metallic minutes clicked past on the big wall clock. Then, the latch of the school door clattered. Rearing forward very slightly in her chair, Deirdre listened to the sound of someone entering. The footsteps, moving like clock-work down the corridor and up the stairs, were neat and tidy-minded. As they neared, Deirdre's eyes narrowed to glinting slits. She exhaled slowly from her cigarette and, through the smoke, smiled as at the first strains of an overture.

The door opened and a rather small heavily clothed woman stepped into the room. Dressed for bad weather though she was, she looked, with her red-cherry cheeks and wide semicircle of smile, like something that might have briskly swung out of a weather-house predicting sunshine.

'Oh, goodness, Mrs Blain,' she almost sang, 'you are bright and early. I thought I'd be the first as usual. But you've beaten me to it.'

As she spoke, she was busy putting away her umbrella and untying a transparent plastic rain-hood that she was wearing over a rayon head-square.

Deirdre said in her flat voice—it had slightly less energy and slightly less volume that most people's—'I thought I'd make an effort to start the term off well.'

'Yes, indeed.' Agnes Lilley had now perched on the edge of a chair and, still in her nylon mac, was undoing the polythene rain-boots she pulled over her Hush Puppies on muddy days. 'And you've had a good holi-day, I hope.'

'So-so.' Deirdre tapped at her cigarette, carefully scattering ash over the face of the Virgin of Fatima. 'How about you?'

She looked at her attentively. Agnes, who had just hung up her blue nylon mac, was in the process of unbuttoning her coat. As she did this, she said to Deirdre, 'Oh, I mustn't complain. It was very pleasant— especially the trip with the girls to the Sisters at Broadstairs. They gave us a lovely time, as Carmel will have told you.' She paused, fingering one of her round buttons. 'But, well, I don't know if you've heard but, a week or so ago. . . .'

'Yes, how is your father?' asked Deirdre, her eyes browsing around Agnes' face.

'Rather poorly, I'm afraid. He's in intensive care at the moment. And—oh, I suppose we can only say our prayers, can't we?'

'You must really be feeling it,' said Deirdre and drew on her cigarette, not letting her eyes leave Agnes.

'Yes, well, I am upset, of course. But people have been very good. They always are. You just wouldn't believe.'

'No,' said Deirdre.

'Mother Monica's got the whole convent making a novena—so if that doesn't help. . . .' Agnes gave a little laugh and bit her lip, leaving a white mark on its red plumpness for a second. 'And you'd be amazed at the number of Masses people have sent in. It's been wonderful. Eight o'clock, this morning, was said for Daddy, as a matter of fact. And ever so many people turned up. I'm sure it's meant that some of them were late for work.'

'How nice.' Deirdre stubbed out her cigarette with a firm pressure of her nicotine-brown finger.

'It was. It's like Emily was saying to me only last night, it's amazing how much of a consolation your faith is to you at a time like this. How it keeps you going.'

'Yes, it must be a comfort to think that,' said Deirdre.

Agnes looked at her, then carried her coat across to the rack. As she arranged it on its hanger, she said over her cardiganed shoulder, 'Yes, ever so many people were there this morning. And both Carmel and Mr Blain, of course. You know, you're very lucky, Mrs Blain. There can't be many women with a husband like yours. I mean, goodness, he nearly lives in that church, doesn't he?'

'He certainly does,' Deirdre drawled with careful unconcern. She rubbed at the mole on her cheek, then said, 'Of course, I'd like to have got to church myself this morning. But—well, you wouldn't really know—but when you've got a husband and family to see to, there just isn't that much time.'

She lounged across to the window and looked down into the playground.

'I hope the kids are having enough sense to go straight into the hall, this weather,' she said. 'I don't fancy starting the term with wet clothes all over the radiators.'

'Oh, Mr and Mrs Ashworth are down there,' said Agnes, referring to the headmaster and his wife. 'They'll be seeing them in.'

'I certainly hope so,' announced a deeper voice from the doorway. 'There are little terrors splashing around in puddles all over the place. That Maddox girl nearly knocked me off my bicycle.'

Deirdre looked across at Emily Gorshaw, big in her belted Burberry. 'Well,' she said with a weary little mouth-movement, 'the team's all here—ready for the last lap before we all move on to better things. And it's nearly nine o'clock.'

'Yes, and I know I'm on yard and hall duty, this week,' said Emily. 'And I know I'm a bit late—*mea culpa*.' She banged a clenched fist in parody-penitence on her navy-blue gaberdined bust. 'But if Father Fitz's bacon and sausages aren't fried to a frazzle, there's all hell to pay.'

'Emily,' murmured Agnes with a reproving tilt of the head.

'Sorry,' said Emily, comically putting on what she called her Act of Contrition face. 'I'm just pointing out to Mrs Blain that it's no joke trying to be a teacher and a priest's housekeeper—however part-time.'

'Yes,' said Agnes, sending her a solicitous little smile, 'it must be very tiring.'

'It is tiring, looking after a man's fads and fancies. There's nothing more exhausting.' Emily's broad face purpled with hilarity under her wiry bush of steel-grey hair.

'I can certainly appreciate that,' said Deirdre in her listless voice, glancing sideways at Agnes.

'We can all appreciate it,' said Emily. 'You with that husband of yours. Me with Father Fitz. And Agnes here....' She stopped and clapped a meaty hand over her open mouth. 'Oh, laws, I'm sorry, love.'

'It's all right, Emily,' said Agnes. 'I know you meant well.'

'And anyway it's true. You've been a trooper the way you've looked after that dad of yours. There's many a husband, I can tell you, who'd think himself lucky to have a home run like you run yours. That's if men had any sense, I mean.'

She walked with her heavy broad-footed tread across to the cupboard and pulled out a large hand-bell.

'Well, nine o'clock. I'd better go and round up the sheep and the goats.'

She clanked the bell experimentally a couple of times, and, as its reverberations died away, Deirdre murmured, 'Ask not for whom the bell tolls.'

'What?' said Emily.

'It's a quotation—a bit of a sermon. About death and funerals.'

Instantly, Emily's face corrugated into a huge frown of warning. She swivelled her eyes in the direction of Agnes, who was bending, with her back towards them, over her open handbag. 'Her father's very bad,' Emily wide-mouthed at Deirdre and nodded in brusque emphasis. After which, ringing the bell with energetic shakings of her wrist, she strode down the stairs.

Deirdre waited until she was out of earshot. Then, 'Ask not for whom the bell tolls,' she recited again and a little louder. 'It tolls for thee.' And as she stared at Agnes' back, her smile was as big as her mouth could make it.

An hour before the funeral, the bell of Holy Cross began to sound, sending its resonant reminder from the soot-encrusted tower, out through the pallid sunlight, and across the parish. As soon as she heard it, Deirdre raised her head from the newspaper she was reading, stubbed out her cigarette without so much as looking at it, and walked quickly from the kitchen to the living-room. Here, there was a smell of liniment and Brylcreem; a lard-faced man with hair of a colour somewhere between fair and grey was hunched over the table, writing.

'I hope you're nearly ready, Vincent,' Deirdre said to him.

Not taking his pen from the pad or his eyes from what he'd written, her husband replied, in a voice where extreme precision of diction could be heard trying to force its way through nasal congestion, 'I just want to finish this letter to the *Radio Times.* I think somebody ought to say something about that play.'

Deirdre's already thin lips narrowed. 'I know you do,' she said.

'It shouldn't be allowed to pass without comment. They'll try it again, if we don't speak out. And that'd make us as bad as they are. There are sins of omission.'

'Well, write it quickly,' Deirdre said. 'I want us to get off.'

'Why?' Vincent asked mucously as his fountain-pen moved with scratchy deliberation across the stationery. 'What's the hurry?'

'I don't think we should be late,' Deirdre said. 'Not for a funeral.' She paused for a second, massaging the bruise-coloured mole upon her cheek, then added, 'Not for Mr Lilley's funeral.'

'We're not going to be late, though, are we?' Vincent blotted his protest, folded it, and pushed it into an envelope. 'Not unless the church has moved on a few miles since I last saw it.'

He laughed, licked the flap of the envelope with the slightly coated tongue that had emerged during this activity, and then smacked down the flap with a heavy fist-movement as if clinching his point.

The greyish skin round Deirdre's eyes contracted. 'No, but we should be early, Vincent,' she said. 'We should try to get there early.'

Only half-attending as his big white fingers rummaged in his pigskin wallet for a stamp, Vincent asked, 'Whatever for?'

'Out of respect,' Deirdre told him, emphasising the last word in a deliberately priggish way. Then, as her husband, breathily checking the address he had printed on the envelope, still failed to respond, she added rather more loudly, 'And because I want to make sure I get a good seat.'

'A good seat?' Vincent's pink-rimmed eyes blinked across at her at last. 'That's a nice expression to be using of a church.'

'I want to see what little Miss Agnes looks like as a widow.' Deirdre delivered her statement in a casual tone and then went very still, just biting the edge of her lower lip, watching her husband attentively.

In a voice where forbearance was made as audible as possible—though, again, catarrh performed some muting—Vincent said, 'I don't know what you're driving at, Deirdre, and I don't intend to ask. You know as well as I do it's her father who's died.'

'Yes, and I know something else, too. I know that that's the nearest she'll ever come to being a widow.'

For a moment or two, while he ostentatiously let the remark die a decent death, Vincent gazed at her in silence—though his look spoke a familiar message: re-

proach in the slightly swimmy eyes, a striving to forgive
in the gently smiling shape his lips were gradually assum-
ing. It was a look that Deirdre particularly loathed—
'extreme unction' was her private name for it—and one
that, early in their married life, had always goaded her
to strident verbal anger. Years of co-existence, though,
had taught her the advantage of control. When looked at
now in mute rebuke, she no longer raised her voice,
letting her husband keep his unexcited dignity, like
some teetotal do-gooder pityingly witnessing the frenzies
of an alcoholic. Now she kept quiet too until, usually, he
was compelled to speak—compelled quite often, as today,
to try one of his ironies.

'Perhaps you haven't heard,' he said, speaking slowly
through the fixed smile intended to display that he had
not yet lost his temper, 'but somebody once said, "Love
thy neighbour". It does us no harm to remember that
bit of advice from time to time.'

'What a fund of information you are, Vincent,' said
Deirdre, turning away from him.

'I mean,' he continued in his thick catarrh-clogged
tones, 'it might just stop you sneering at a girl who's. . . .'

'"Girl"? Did you say "girl"?' Deirdre swung a faceful
of mockery round at her husband and tilted it aggressive-
ly towards him. 'She's nearly fifty if she's a day, Vincent.
Nearly fifty. We all know old Hector practically kept her
in pigtails and pinafores, but that doesn't mean she's
still. . . .'

'I'm not going to argue with you, Deirdre,' said
Vincent, zipping shut his writing-case. 'Not this morning.
Not before we go to Communion. I have respect for that

sacrament, if you don't. But I will just say this—I think you ought to sit down quietly and ponder those remarks of yours. Just you ask yourself if it's a very Christian thing to do—laughing at a . . . a woman who's just lost her father. And before he's even in his grave.'

'Oh, I am sorry,' Deirdre said with a melodious clarity. 'I was forgetting. I should wait until they've thrown the last shovelful in, shouldn't I? I mean, it'll be all right for me to say what I think then, won't it?'

'I'm beginning to wonder if it'll ever be all right for you to say what you think,' retorted Vincent. 'But there we are.'

Rather laboriously, as though patience were a loaded sack across his shoulders visibly slowing him, he moved on his plump haunches over to the door.

'Carmel,' he called up the stairs in a carefully normal way. 'Aren't you ready yet?'

Turning back into the room, he sneezed and stopped to dab at his runny eyes with a handkerchief.

'Well,' said Deirdre, 'I might leave something to be desired but you're obviously going to be a great asset.'

'What do you mean—an asset?'

'I mean that you look positively grief-stricken.'

'You know very well it's my allergy, it's that rhinitis.'

'Yes,' she giggled. 'You'd better keep away from the Lilleys. They'll really make your eyes water.'

Vincent's candle-coloured skin flushed with new exasperation. 'Look, Deirdre, I've just said. We're going to church and we're going to Communion. At least I am. I think you'd better ask yourself whether you're in a fit state to approach those altar-rails. . . .'

He had begun to raise his voice but, as their daughter Carmel came into the room, immediately swerved it back towards pleasantness.

'And here's Carmel,' he said, 'so I'll just go and take my drops, and then we can get off.'

As they waited for him to return, Deirdre glanced across at her daughter, slender in a dark-grey flannel coat: and briefly some contentment ironed tension from her face. The black velvet hood that Carmel had borrowed from a friend to wear for the funeral threw into very good relief her soft fair hair, clear skin still warmed from summer sun, and impressively wide pansy-brown eyes.

'You look nice, love,' Deirdre said. 'I thought that hat would be a bit on the dismal side, but it suits you.'

Instantly, a deep blush flooded up the girl's smooth cheeks, around her eyes, and to her forehead.

'Oh, Mummy,' she said. 'We're going to a funeral. You shouldn't talk like that.'

'Now, don't get into one of your states,' said Deirdre. 'There's no need. You hardly ever saw old Hector Lilley, so don't start carrying on as if you're in mourning for your nearest and dearest. It'd be hypocritical.'

Again the girl blushed, her cheeks visibly going hot.

'I'm not so upset about Mr Lilley,' she answered indignantly. 'I never said I was. I'm not a hypocrite. You always make things sound nasty.'

'Oh, stop it, Carmel,' said Deirdre curtly. 'If you're not upset, then that's that. Let the matter drop.'

'I am upset. I'm upset for Miss Lilley. It must be awful for her. He was all she'd got in the whole world.'

'Oh, Agnes Lilley'll survive, don't you worry.'

'I keep thinking how terrible it is. She was so nice to us on holiday. And then, as soon as she arrived back, this happened.'

'What happened, love?' Vincent walked back into the room, carrying his own and Deirdre's coat.

'Mr Lilley dying.'

'Yes, it's a sad thing, is that.' Vincent's voice went particularly breathy as he struggled into his coat, then loudened again. 'You see, you never really knew what he was like, Carmel. You only saw him when he was old. But he taught me, you know. He was my headmaster. And your mother's.'

'I know. And I think they should make Miss Lilley headmistress because of that. It's only fair. She's his daughter.'

'There'd not be much point in making her headmistress of a school that's closing down at Christmas,' Deirdre said with some exasperation. 'Use your sense.'

'Then they should make her headmistress at the new school, Maria Goretti. It might make up to her for her father.'

'Don't be so foolish, Carmel,' Deirdre said sharply. 'You know perfectly well it's going to be run by nuns. We've already got a headmistress—Mother Monica. There'll be precious few lay-teachers on the staff of that school, let alone in charge of it. We shall all need to keep on the right side of Mother Monica, I can tell you. If we want to hold on to our jobs.'

'Don't dramatise, Deirdre,' said Vincent.

'It's not drama. I wish it was. It's plain blunt fact. There are going to be redundancies because of this rearrangement, you know. More teachers have been given their notice than have been taken on at Maria Goretti. And that woman knows it. She's got us all on a term's probation. Right in the palm of her hand. And people like me with sick husbands can't afford to join the dole queue, can we?'

'Oh, really, Deirdre,' Vincent protested. 'I'd remind you that you're talking about nuns, not a protection racket.'

'Daddy,' asked Carmel, 'do you think Miss Lilley might become a nun now?'

'Oh, well, it's not for us to say, is it, love? Vocations come from God. It's not a thing you just decide for yourself. There has to be a call. As I know,' he added with a significant look.

'I think she'd like it as a nun. She liked it at Broadstairs. We all did. It was really good fun, not dismal and serious like you might think.'

'Yes, it's funny how people get hold of the wrong idea about religion,' said Vincent. 'How they don't see that it's a joyful thing. They always have this notion that nuns and priests are miserable.'

'The Sisters weren't,' said Carmel. 'They weren't a bit miserable. It was like being in a nice big family.'

'Yes, well, think of the name,' said Vincent, ponderously lowering his pale face towards her. '"Sisters"—it tells you what they are.'

'Yes,' Carmel nodded, 'and the head nun's called Mother.'

'To show they're all one family.'

Carmel was silent for a moment, then said, 'I wish I'd

had some real sisters. Of my own. Why didn't I?'

'It wasn't possible,' said Deirdre very rapidly. After the difficult birth of Carmel, she had had a hysterectomy—much to the horror and indignation of Vincent, who would now, she knew, be giving her his God-is-not-mocked look. Keeping her eyes away from him, she firmly continued, 'Anyway, come on, we're going to be late.'

With the funeral bell sounding like a vibrant canopy above their heads, they began to climb the gradual hill to Holy Cross church. As they did so, Carmel pressed her father for more information about Hector Lilley. What was he like when he was young? Was he as good a teacher as Miss Lilley? Was he as nice as she was?

'He was a very fine Catholic gentleman, that's what he was,' said Vincent. 'One of the old school. He set an example and he proclaimed his faith. Every Saturday morning, come rain or come shine, he was down on the Market, speaking for the Catholic Evidence Guild. Putting the case.' He shook his head in admiration. 'And the way he ran that school—well, heaven help you if you didn't know your catechism inside out. It was different from what it is now. Of course, I'm not saying anything about Mr Ashworth—don't get me wrong. But he's not had it in him. Not the way Hector Lilley did.' After a little ruminative chewing of his lower lip, he went on, 'But, then, it was all different in those days. It was different at the church as well. Stricter, you know. None of this letting things slide. I mean, many's the time I've seen women turned away from those Communion-rails in tears because they went to receive the Blessed Sacrament with lipstick on their mouths. There was no painting up for Dean Delaney. And there was no sloppy business for Hector Lilley either.'

Irritated by Vincent's insistent voice and the sight of Carmel's open face, so wastefully attentive and receptive, Deirdre dropped behind a pace or two. As she walked, with head a little to one side and hands in the patch-pockets of her coat, she tried to control her annoyance—Deirdre disliked betraying anger in front of her daughter—and, to distract her mind, sent it back through its dossier on Hector Lilley.

For almost as long as Deirdre could remember, he had looked more or less the same—a stocky little figure with hair the colour of white pepper and eyes as red as if some of it had got into them. His face, pushed several inches forward by an aggressive jut of the neck, was quite regularly crimsoned to some degree of rage. She could see him now storming, every Monday morning, at the five Caunce children from Bengal Street because they had not got their mother to take them to Sunday Mass. She could hear the big frayed cane slapping into the palm of some stammering pupil who hadn't been able to remember the Corporal Works of Mercy or who had got mixed up trying to recite the Twelve Fruits of the Holy Ghost. She could recall Hector outside school as well—standing in the Market on a wooden crate haranguing passers-by in a barking voice while his sandy-haired hands gestured fiercely with the pamphlets they were clutching: he was known as Tiger Lilley to some of the locals. She could even remember odd details like the smell of snuff coming from his heavy tweed suit when, at Aunt Edith's insistence, she had asked him to sign her autograph album, the day she left school. 'This is the motto of Holy Cross—Work hard, play hard, pray hard', he had inscribed, blackly underlining the last two words with the broad nib of his sturdy bakelite fountain-pen.

Deirdre could remember, too, that Hector had never really liked her, just as he had never liked her mother. Gertrude's legs had been slapped many times by those pamphlet-brandishing hands, slapped until they were mottled and bloodshot, Aunt Edith used to claim: not that that had stopped them getting into mischief and silk stockings soon enough. Deirdre he had only slapped once—stingingly, across the face, for laughing when he was telling them the story of St Simeon Stylites.

Vincent, who had attended the school some years before her, had never been chastised. Hector had very much approved of him and his breathy docilities. It was Hector, really, who had got Vincent off to the seminary. And here, as Deirdre strolled, her mind opened another file, one with which she was much more familiar.

She thought, again, of Vincent at the seminary—of the numerous accounts she had heard, especially in their earlier days, of his life there: reminiscences that always led to the climax of his failure—his ultimate and conscientious inability to become a priest. The official reason for this had been that his health would not stand up to it: after the illness when his lung collapsed, Vincent never returned to the seminary. But, as he had explained to Deirdre with some earnest excitement, it had not just been a question of respiratory disorder. He had also—a more painful thing—developed scruples. He had worried through long dormitory nights about his worthiness: had worried himself back into the outside world again, where his inflamed nerves cooled. But the anxiety never entirely lapsed. After a certain amount of time, there would be re-eruptions, scruples breaking out again. Vincent would begin to spend excessive time in the confessional, would find it worryingly hard to keep his mind upon his prayers, could even have guilt feelings about carelessly swallowing, on meat-forbidden Friday, a shred of stewed steak that had lodged in a cranny of his teeth after Thursday's supper.

Why, Deirdre would wonder even more bitterly than usual during these phases, had she ever married him? And in miserable litany the drab responses came: because she had been desperate to get away from Aunt Edith and that statue-crammed house; because no other man had shown any sign of interest in her; because—meeting him at a teachers' training college dance—she had assumed that Vincent Blain, having left the seminary, would gradually become less and less religious, rather as a recuperating invalid, getting out and about again, slowly loses pallor.

Well, it had not worked out like that. Vincent had remained religious. Priestly mannerisms clung to him like the smell of candle-wax and incense. And especially in church he sounded like a seminarian, praying more loudly and more slowly than anyone else, so that, at the end of a prayer, his voice, reverently a couple of words behind, would sonorously move with unembarrassed public piety to the concluding 'Amen'.

Vincent had not even become, as intended, a teacher.

His first term in a boys' grammar school put him in a convalescent home. After which his doctor advised him to try something less taxing. It was one of Vincent's little jokes that this recommendation eventually led him to the Inland Revenue office, where he now worked—though only part-time, as his ill-health made him unreliable.

The leisure that this gave him he devoutly filled with work for the church—it was another of his jokes that he served both God and Caesar. When he wasn't checking the tax returns, Vincent was helping Father Fitzgerald with the parish accounts or giving a hand to Miss Lilley and Miss Gorshaw if the hymn-books needed mending. He ran the altar-boys' guild, and frequently served Mass himself, moving respectfully around the sanctuary with a special cushion-footed gait. He also went round the parish, once a week, delivering the football coupon, and, once a month, delivering *The Word*, a missionary magazine.

Two days ago, on an evening of sudden rain, he had returned, drenched to his scapular, after one of these paper-rounds, as he called them.

'Well, it's nice, isn't it?' Deirdre said bitterly as he sat drinking tea in his dressing-gown, his wet clothes steaming round the fire. 'It's nice—you getting yourself into that state, and all for nothing. Not a penny.'

'I'm not interested in earthly rewards, Deirdre,' he had said, holding the cup in both his hands and gazing down at the beige liquid.

'No, but I am. Somebody's got to keep this house going. And it'll not be you, will it?—coughing and spluttering and probably ready to have another week off work. What do you think would happen if I was ill or lost my job?'

Vincent smiled. 'Remember the marriage feast at Cana, Deirdre? All that fretting, and there was no need, was there? Because the Lord provided.'

The anger Deirdre had experienced then percolated through into her present bitterness, fortifying it. As she caught up with Vincent and Carmel just outside the church, she could feel the rage inside her pushing for some outlet—spasmodically fluttering a muscle under her right eye, causing her fingernails to dig a little into her moist palms.

'Well, here we are,' said Vincent, 'and that's Hector Lilley for you, Carmel.'

'He sounds marvellous,' the girl said. 'But Miss Lilley's daddy would be bound to be nice.'

'Bless you,' said Vincent, tapping his daughter's biscuit-coloured cheek with one of his limp sausage-shaped white fingers. He smiled at her and then at Deirdre.

They had reached the church door and, as Vincent quietly opened it, Deirdre coughed savagely. Trying to keep the anger from her voice but feeling it pulse around her temples, she whispered, 'Make sure you find us a bench where we can see, Vincent. But not too near the coffin. Remember what it says in that poem about Lilleys that fester.'

Father Fitzgerald had circled the coffin sprinkling it with holy water: drops still glittered on the dark and polished wood. Rhythmically, robed in black, and standing between the brown wax candles used for funerals, he had swung the silver thurible around it. White-grey incense fumes now circled slowly up in vaporous intercession, as they had so often done throughout the many Benedictions and High Masses of Agnes Lilley's life. It was almost time for the body to be carried out, past the Lourdes Grotto, to the graveyard: buried where three generations of the family—remembered every year in the prayers and Masses of the November Death List—already lay. But before the procession left the church, Father Fitzgerald, reassuring in his requiem vestments, gave what both bereaved Miss Lilley and upset Miss Gorshaw afterwards agreed was a most consoling sermon, the sort of thing that made you realise you were lucky to be a Catholic and have something to hold on to.

He wanted to stress, he said, that this was not a sad occasion—though, of course, it was a time of grief, very understandable grief at the loss of an exemplary Catholic, a fine headmaster, and—his rimless spectacles, catching the morning light, glinted briefly towards Miss Lilley—an extraordinary father. But this was only transient: temporary grief at a temporary separation. There would one day, as they all sitting in that church knew to their comfort, be certain reunion. And just as our joy in meeting a friend can be increased an hundredfold if we have not seen him for some time—is there not the proverb 'Absence makes the heart grow fonder'?—so in heaven there will be even greater joy as separated loved ones reunite and God wipes away all tears. Not that there was any need for tears, said Father Fitzgerald, raising his already pulpit-volumed voice. It would be wrong to think of Hector Lilley as dead. He was alive, more fully alive than he had ever been—than any of us ever could be in this life. It was no longer through a glass darkly that he saw but face to face. A good man—and if ever there was a man who never shrank from openly, nay eagerly, proclaiming his faith, it was Hector Lilley—a good man had gone to collect his just and earned reward. Why should they feel gloomy about that? His faith, as they all well knew, had been Hector Lilley's comfort and his strength whilst he was amongst them. He would have been the first to wish that it should be both these things to his survivors now that he was gone.

After this address—during which Agnes Lilley's handkerchief continually visited her nose and eyes—the choir began to sing 'Faith of our fathers', Mr Lilley's favourite hymn, while six officials from the Men's Guild lifted his coffin off its stand and carried it, wobbling slightly on their suited shoulders, down the centre aisle. The carved figures in the Stations of the Cross—Veronica, Simon of Cyrene, Jesus Meeting his Afflicted Mother—looked down at Agnes Lilley with their wooden eyes as they had done ever since she was a girl. Trying not to cry, she kept close to Emily Gorshaw. In front of them the men moved slowly, their footsteps becoming suddenly louder as they left the linoleum of the church floor for the stone flags of its big cold porch. Carefully, getting ready for the turn, they made their way between the baptismal font and the repository-stall—manned every Sunday, after Mass, by Emily Gorshaw, but today locked and shrouded under dust-covers.

The service was almost over and, with some relief, Agnes Lilley recognised that she had not really broken down, had not made the kind of weak exhibition of herself that her father would have tongue-lashed as soft acting, silly nonsense, women's carry-on. For just a moment, seeing the men from the Guild march down the middle aisle—as her father had done in his best suit, holding the collection-plate, every Sunday until his last illness—she had felt her throat contract, her eyes brim, and her mouth convulse with hurt. But then the familiarity of the church and ritual, the cadences of prayers she had been saying now for nearly half a century, soothed away her pain.

As she stepped out from the darker church into the pale September light, Emily put an arm through hers. Together they moved into the cemetery where old Mr Calderbank, who dug the graves, was standing respectfully, flat cap in leathery hand, to watch the burial.

It was soon over. More prayers were said as, ropes straining and planks creaking round the open grave, the coffin was lowered. Earth from the priest's chalky fingers pattered on its lid. Momentarily, again, tears blurred Agnes Lilley's eyes. Everything distorted into glinting fragments of wet sight, then she blinked, clearing her vision, and in the first instant of new clarity saw Deirdre Blain standing opposite, not lowering her head as most of the people were but staring hard at her, staring very fixedly. Vincent Blain, his eyes red and his lips moving in prayer, was next to her. Slightly behind them was Carmel, holding a prayer-book. And there were the nuns

from the convent, and the teachers from the new boys'
secondary school, which had been closed that morning
out of respect. A brisk tug on Agnes' arm pulled her
attention round to Emily, who whispered, 'Come on,
love, we'll go and find that taxi.' As she was led away,
Agnes heard behind her Deirdre's cough, and heavier
loads of soil beginning to drum down, shovelled heftily
in by Mr Calderbank.

Pounding on the table with the flat of her big hand,
Emily Gorshaw called for order. As the talking died
down into silence, she announced, 'Now, look, I don't
want to spoil the fun, and the social's not over yet. But
in case any of our very welcome guests start trying to
slip away unnoticed now that it's getting later, I just
want to say a big Holy Cross thank-you to them all—
thank you for coming along and thank you for adding
to the gaiety.' Her brick-complexioned face, having
grinned and nodded round the room, now became mock-
serious. 'And in case any of you girls start slipping away,
I want to remind you that it's the Guild Communion,
next Sunday. So don't forget, eight o'clock sharp. And
let's see you all with those green ribbons round your
necks for once, so that we really look like a Guild—and
put the Children of Mary to shame,' she added, beaming
friendly rivalry at Agnes Lilley.

It was All Souls' Night, the last evening in October,
and inside the parish hall, where dusty heat beat vig-
orously from the pipes and radiators, members of the
Guild of Saint Agnes were holding a Hallowe'en social.
It was an occasion Deirdre would normally have shunned:

but hearing that a party of nuns from the convent would be bringing some visiting novices along, had thought it prudent to attend. Until her probation at the new school was safely behind her, she needed to miss no opportunity of showing Mother Monica that she was satisfactory: as the thought of Vincent, just down with his first bout of winter flu, glumly reminded her.

The social had been very much as Deirdre had anticipated. They had had their supper, eating at long trestle-tables under lurid-shaded lights. They had listened to ghost stories, sipping lemonade or tea. One of the nuns had given a short talk on spirits and possession. They had played at bob-the-apple and a game devised by Agnes Lilley called 'Hallowe'en Consequences'. There had also been a dressing-up competition, with a prize, for the 'most sinister crone'. 'I hope they've told Mother Monica that professionals aren't allowed to enter,' Deirdre had murmured, causing Carmel's face to kindle. Uncharmed, she had sat and watched while the girls, dressed and made up as hags, had stumped around the room, theatrically brandishing their fingernails at people. 'Heavens!' Agnes Lilley kept protesting, 'aren't they gruesome!'

No, thought Deirdre, but the evening was. Trying to count her blessings, she reminded herself that, once she had got her contract at Maria Goretti, she could firmly turn her back on such occasions. And after Christmas, marvellously, too, she could turn her back on both Agnes Lilley and Emily Gorshaw, neither of whom was moving to the new school. Emily had decided to withdraw from teaching altogether and throw all her energies into priest's housekeeping; Agnes was going to a local junior school.

It was this that most pleased Deirdre—never to have to work with Agnes Lilley again, never to have to listen to that relentlessly bright voice chirping on, above the click of knitting-needles, about joy and patience and wasn't Father's sermon lovely and how those Goan nuns had sent a really nice letter in gratitude for the donation and oh, thank goodness, it was only two weeks to the end of Lent and then she could go back to having sugar in her tea, not to mention eating sweets, and had Mrs Blain noticed how that stained-glass window of the Entry into Jerusalem always caught the sunlight during Bene-diction? Just occasionally, Deirdre had managed to staunch some of the saccharine, had provoked Agnes towards a show of temper. But, exasperatingly, she had never needled her to open aggression. Always, Agnes stopped herself, turning the other lightly powdered cheek with enraging meekness, murmuring, 'We're getting rather heated, aren't we, Mrs Blain, so I suggest we just agree to differ. And, anyway, if you'll excuse me, I really must go and sort the tidy-boxes.' Even her father's death had not dimmed her tinsel. Contrary to Deirdre's eager hopes, she had cheerfully weathered it, had been 'a little champion' in the frequently aired opinion of Emily Gorshaw, who increasingly spent her spare time round at the bungalow, keeping Agnes company.

Agnes and Emily were talking now together—'having a confab' as Emily usually called it—in the centre of the hall. Irritatedly clearing her throat, Deirdre listened to their laughter, the girlish peal of the one, the mannish guffaw of the other. Probably, after Emily's speech, they would be exchanging some predictable ribbing—Emily was president of the Guild of Saint Agnes, to which the younger girls belonged; Agnes of the Children of Mary, which they joined when slightly older. It was a joke of Emily's that there were two guilds for young women in the parish—the Guild of Saint Agnes and the Guild of Miss Agnes: 'Though, after the way you looked after that dad of yours,' she'd sometimes gruffly mutter, 'I don't know why we don't say Saint for both and be done with it.'

Or perhaps, Deirdre thought with another wince of resentment, they were talking about the foreign holidays that, unlike her, they could afford. Not, she told herself in sour consolation, that they ever made much of it. Agnes' holidays were most often spent at Lourdes: every other year, she went as a handmaiden to help with the sick, and, as the White Train sped towards the Pyrenees with its ill and hopeful cargo, circulated with her smile and patience. On the years when she did not go to Lourdes, Agnes branched out, as Deirdre gibingly put it to herself, had a change and toured the shrines of France, visited Fatima, or Rome when it was Holy Year, or Munich for the Eucharistic Congress.

Emily was quite widely travelled, too, returning, laughing, from her various holy wanderings and with riotous accounts of comic foreign mishap: that time in the Baths at Lourdes when her elastic went, or how she'd lost her bottom set in a hotel in Oberammergau, when there for the Passion Play, and the young chambermaid not able to understand a single word she said—laws, she'd been in fits and nearly burst her corsets hooting when she told the girls about it over their glasses of apple-juice. 'Emily!' Agnes would sometimes pinkly murmur during these tales. But, like someone on a strict diet allowing herself the occasional doughnut, Emily would grin and carry on: Mass every day and keeping the presbytery going earned her the right to make the odd 'broad' reference.

Still laughing, the two women walked over to a group of novices and girls, amongst whom was Carmel. Looking across at her, Deirdre, for a moment, felt a rare sense of pleasure, for a moment pondered the unexpected good fortune—that Carmel should resemble neither her nor Vincent but, of all people, Gertrude. Not that the girl's face was exactly like that smiling out from Aunt Edith's few faded photographs. Innocuous-eyed, Carmel looked more tractable than obviously eager Gertrude. But still the girl did have Gertrude's good features and slanting attractive smile. And with them, Deirdre hoped, she would find herself a worthwhile husband and escape from everything that she was trapped among. It would be worth it, she often felt nowadays, watching Carmel mature; it would be worth all the long payment of her marriage for her daughter to do well and get away; it would be compensation.

Glancing at her watch, Deirdre saw with relief that it was almost half past ten; she could decently leave. She crossed the polished floor to where her daughter sat, bright-eyed and laughing.

'Come on, Carmel,' she said. 'Time for home.'

'Oh, Mummy, not yet. . . .'

'Home, Carmel. Your father'll be waiting.'

'Must she, Mrs Blain?' Agnes Lilley took hold of Carmel's sleeve as if expecting that they would enter into some playful tug-of-war.

'Yes, can't we plead for her?' asked one of the novices, a raw-faced and nervily jolly girl. 'We'll see she doesn't get into any mischief.'

Deirdre's voice took on an even more decided note. 'No,' she said. 'Definitely not. Her father's ill. He's at home, waiting. We must get back.'

It did not take them long to do this, the Blains' house being only a street or so away from the parish hall. As they hurried along the windy pavements, Deirdre said to Carmel, 'I don't know why you made such a song and dance about leaving. It can't have been very exciting listening to a bunch of nuns and their chatter.'

In a surprisingly firm voice, Carmel replied, 'I liked it. It was interesting. Bernadette—that's one of the novices. . . .'

'The big girl with the spots?'

'Bernadette told me all sorts of things about the novitiate.'

'With that thick Irish accent, I'm surprised you didn't need an interpreter.'

By-passing the remark, Carmel opened the gate. Vincent—in his dressing-gown, a scarf around his neck—had come to the door, and stood, smiling, in the porch. Running towards him, Carmel shouted, 'Oh, I've had a marvellous time, Daddy. Some of the girls from Broadstairs were there and. . . .'

*

On the first day of the last week, Deirdre Blain was early once again. Not taking off her winter coat, she moved over to the staff-room window and gazed out through glass and frost towards some distant roofs, now white with ice and only partly visible through a freezing fog. At least, her colour-blenched face and black-smudged eyes were turned in this direction: her attention was elsewhere, obsessively replaying the events of the week-end.

It was now two days since Carmel had announced that she wanted to become a nun; two days since Deirdre—alone with her at first, as Vincent was away upon retreat—had started her struggle to prevent this. She had reasoned, she had argued, she had threatened and cajoled. But Carmel, who had mainly cried, had kept repeating through her sobs that it was a sin to say no if God called you, that she knew she ought to be a nun, that she was going to go to Broadstairs and become one.

'Well, let me tell you, Carmel,' Deirdre had almost hissed at her, 'a holiday in a convent's one thing and being there for good's another.'

'It would just be better,' Carmel said, 'because it would be longer.'

'Don't be so stupid. If you think I'm going to let you throw away your life. . . .'

'It's not throwing it away. It's dedicating it. Miss Lilley says. . . .'

'Don't mention that woman's name to me. I know she's behind all this.'

'I think we should agree to differ, Mummy.'

Deirdre stood still. 'What did you say?'

'I said we should agree to differ. We're just getting angry and. . . .'

Deirdre slapped her hard across the face, leaving upon her cheek a scarlet mark, which then dissolved into the blush that slowly welled around it.

'Don't parrot that woman's words to me.'

Carmel had collapsed into a chair, weeping with her face against the cushion.

'Listen,' Deirdre touched her heaving shoulder. 'You're not old enough to decide something like this yet, Carmel. I know you like Miss Lilley. And I shouldn't have hit you. But there are things you don't really understand.'

'I do understand.' The voice came smothered from the cushion.

'Carmel, you don't. Now, listen to me. Agnes Lilley hasn't ever led a proper life. You can't put any trust in what she says.'

'I think you're awful saying that. She's always nice and happy. Not like you.'

Deirdre rubbed furiously at the mole upon her cheek as if trying to peel it off.

'What she tells you is silly and naïve. You'll ruin your life if you listen to that sentimental stuff.'

'I want to be a nun.'

'But, Carmel, think of what you'll be missing. Don't you want to get married?'

'I will be getting married. I'll be the Bride of Christ.'

'Don't talk nonsense.'

'It's not nonsense. Bernadette told me. You wear a wedding-dress. . . .'

'And walk down the aisle by yourself. And spend your honeymoon amongst a bunch of silly women.'

'I'm not going to listen to you,' Carmel said defiantly, and looking up with raw red smudges round her big wet eyes. 'You're saying wicked things. Miss Lilley said there'd be temptations, and I'd have to get round obstacles and persevere.'

They had both persevered—arguing and shouting—until Vincent arrived back from his retreat. His first reaction had, of course, been one of sheer delight. 'I can hardly believe it,' he kept saying. 'I thought I was in the wilderness, but I've been making straight the path. Can't you see the pattern, Deirdre? I thought I'd let God down— but, all the time, he was working in his mysterious way. And now it all adds up. The Church lost me but it's got Carmel. It's a kind of compensation.'

That was before they went to Sunday Mass where, by a stroke of luck, the sermon dealt with spiritual pride. Desperately, Deirdre clutched at Father Fitzgerald's inadvertent straw. All the way home, all the afternoon and evening, she worked on Vincent's scruples, trying to inflame them. Yes, she admitted, she had been hasty; no, she shouldn't have reacted so extremely: but couldn't Vincent see why? It was just that she didn't want Carmel to repeat his mistake, to suffer what he'd been through.

'Vincent, she's too young yet,' Deirdre said. 'We ought to wait until we're absolutely sure that it's what's required of us. It would be a sin to push her. It would be presumptuous. You shouldn't just assume that Carmel's meant to take your place. It would be thinking that you were infallible. It could be spiritual pride.'

Slowly, Vincent weakened and worried. 'There might be something in that,' he began to say. 'You're right that I jumped to conclusions. It does all need more prayer and meditation.'

At last, late on Sunday evening, after Vincent had been to Benediction and stayed in the church an anxious hour, Deirdre won her concession. He agreed that he had been hasty, perhaps even presumptuous—'saying aloud what I thought God's purposes were'. He agreed, as Deirdre coughed painfully in her talk-inflamed throat, that Carmel should not be allowed to enter the novitiate for at least two more years. Not until she had taken her examinations would they let her decide.

The next morning, Carmel looking feverish and exhausted, Deirdre insisted that she stay away from school. 'There's no point your going back this week,' she said. 'No, don't argue. You stay at home and get well so that you can start the new term properly at Maria Goretti.'

And so that you're out of Agnes Lilley's interfering way, she had grimly thought, and was still thinking in the icy staff-room when the clockwork footsteps, making their familiar noise along the corridor, pulled her from her reverie and swung her round to face the door. It opened gently. Agnes Lilley, woollied and scarfed and packed inside a black fur coat, walked neatly in. She looked like some benevolent rodent from a children's story-book.

'Oh, Mrs Blain,' she said, 'what a surprise.'

Not speaking, Deirdre nodded curtly at her.

'Goodness,' Agnes continued, 'you haven't even lit the fire. No wonder you're shivering.' Then she peered anxiously at Deirdre and asked, 'There's nothing wrong, is there, Mrs Blain? You look quite poorly.'

'No, there's nothing wrong,' said Deirdre. 'Everything's all right.'

'Well, I'm glad. Because you don't look at all well. You look as though you've been under strain.'

Deirdre said, 'I've had a harassing weekend, that's all. Carmel's been making a bit of a nuisance of herself, but it's over now.'

'Carmel? A nuisance? Oh, now, Mrs Blain, I can hardly believe that. She's such a sweet girl, docile.'

'Well, she hasn't been this weekend.'

Agnes' face looked worried. 'Oh dear,' she said, 'I'm sorry to hear that. I hope she's not showing signs of being stubborn because that's one of the things a nun just can't be. Poverty, chastity, and *obedience*—that's what Carmel will have to accept now she's going to be a nun.'

Deirdre moved towards her. 'What do you mean—now she's going to be a nun?'

Agnes' face went flustered. 'I hope I haven't spoken out of turn,' she said, fiddling nervously with the cuff of her coat. 'But, surely, she does want to be a nun. I know you'll prefer to keep it secret until everything's quite settled. But she has spoken to me about it, you know.' She smiled at Deirdre. 'I've given her advice. I've done what I could.'

'Yes, I'm sure you have,' said Deirdre.

'And of course the secret's safe with me. I'd never dream of telling anyone. That's your prerogative. You've had all the work of bringing her up, so it's only right that you should be the one who reaps the wonderful reward. A mother's proudest moment. I'm so happy for you, Mrs Blain.'

'Carmel's not going to be a nun,' said Deirdre through straight lips.

Agnes gasped, 'Not going to be a nun?'

'No. Vincent and I think she's too young—that she should wait a few more years.'

'Oh dear,' said Agnes, putting a hand to her pink throat. 'Oh dear me.'

'There's no need to feel sorry,' said Deirdre. 'We don't.'

'It's just that I'm a little worried about what I've done.'

'What you've done?'

'Yes, well, I know I've taken things upon myself a bit. And I suppose it could be seen as interfering. . . .'

'It was interfering,' Deirdre said. 'Stuffing a girl's head full of your ideas. Telling her what to do with her life. Hoping you could. . . .'

'Oh dear, I always sound so muddled when I'm nervous. But, you see, I must apologise.'

'Yes,' said Deirdre harshly, 'and what for? Come on, let's have it. Speak the truth for once.'

Agnes blinked at her. 'I really don't understand, Mrs Blain. You seem cross already and I haven't even told you.'

'Told me what?'

'Well,' Agnes gulped and pulled her plump-lipped mouth into a nervous shape. 'I'm afraid I have a confession to make. Oh dear, I hope it doesn't cause any trouble. But, you see, I spoke to Mother Monica about young Carmel, last night. I thought it would help, you know, speed things up. And she was so interested. Really pleased. I mean, it's not every day there's a vocation in the parish. She said she thought we should get things moving as soon as possible. She wants to have an interview with Carmel. And she's coming here to see you, this afternoon. At two o'clock,' she added.

Deirdre coughed—a tearing noise that sounded as if it must have hurt her throat. But, with glowing eyes, Agnes continued, 'Of course, I know—as you've often reminded me—I'm not a mother. So I don't suppose I really understand these things. But I did think it was all for the best. Carmel really seemed to know her mind. And after all, it's not as though a convent's a prison. She could leave at any time if she found she couldn't make all the sacrifices that the Sisters have to. It's a hard life and they give up so much, don't they? So very much. But then they have their faith to sustain them.' Agnes looked down for a moment at the syrup-coloured toes of her chunky suede bootees; then, slowly raising her eyes, she said, 'As we all do. Our faith—our comfort and our stay, our sword and our strength.' And in front of Deirdre's stricken face, a big ripe smile crept up into her cheeks.

Barbara's Names

DERWENT MAY

WHEN my sister was twelve, she threw off her old names
and took some new ones. Names were her passion that
year. She had a box of about a hundred paper dolls, cut
out of my mother's magazines, or 'books' as we called
them: girls in every variety of gymslip, or jumper and
skirt, with ankle-socks, buttoned shoes and velours hats—
the monotonous girls' fashions of 1943. All these girls
had names, which were written in a school register, and
they were laid out in tight-packed rows on the sitting-
room table for lessons. They answered to their names,
and would even put up their hands and say, 'Can I be
excused, miss?'; they would then be taken under the
table while my sister produced a hiss. She remembered
what all of them were called—the Lucys, Laurels, Bettes,
Veronicas, Valeries—though when they were first cut
out, they had their names written on their backs in blue
ink, which sometimes showed through and stained their
clothes. My sister used this as grounds for telling them
off. She would spend hours with these girls: I'd go out on
my bike after breakfast on a Saturday morning, and find
her still playing with them, my mother complaining
because she couldn't lay the table, when I came back
home at one.

Her own name was Barbara Elizabeth Ellen (mine was

Brian Arthur—our surname was Cotton). 'Brian and Barbara': my mother often used to remark how nice they sounded together. What my father thought of them, I didn't know. He called me 'old man', usually, and my sister 'Nan'. But I had only seen him once, on leave, in the last three years, and he was in north Africa now.

Barbara was dark-haired, stocky, erratic. She'd started, like me, at the local school, then, when she was eleven, she'd begged to go to a cheap private school with red blazers, not far from us, because a friend of hers was going there. My father had squeezed together enough to send her there—attentive to her whims, rather than to her education, knowing he was just off overseas again. We all supposed she'd not bothered in the scholarship exams for the grammar school because she wanted to be with her friend: she denied it, and just said she couldn't do them. A year later, she hated the private school and was back at the local school, with a still better friend. Her dolls' school, with its private school ways, seemed to satisfy her ambitions even more than the real thing.

I was fifteen by the time she changed her names, and in the fifth form at the grammar school in a town three miles away, where I'd gone on the scholarship. My father was a quick-witted but unqualified bank clerk, my mother had been a lady's maid. For some people in the village, I was probably an expression of social change— even an instrument of social change. To me, my life had all seemed perfectly natural.

The friend for whom Barbara had gone back to her old school was another dark-haired girl called Evelyn. (Barbara always preferred girls who looked like her.)

They would often sit together in a wardrobe with the door shut, then come out of it calling each other by new fancy names. But Barbara's big opportunity came to her quite unexpectedly. Evelyn was going to be confirmed, and Barbara wanted to be confirmed at the same time. This brought up the fact that she had not been baptised. My parents had moved just after I was born, and had always meant to take Barbara back to be christened in the church they'd been married in. But the vicar they wanted had been ill for a long time, then he'd died; and gradually the whole business of the baptism had been forgotten.

When she realised she could say her own names at the baptism service for those of riper years, Barbara went half-crazy with excitement. She made her intention known straight away: she was not keeping any of the names she hated. One day, my mother and I were having tea and talking about her. Barbara and I still had a big tea at half past five—I usually had three slices of bread and butter, with tomatoes or meat paste or tinned salmon, which was cheap in the war. Anything more to eat before we went to bed, like a fried sausage, was still at that time an exception, and a treat. That day, Barbara was late back because she'd gone to see the vicar after school. My mother was very upset about what she wanted to do.

'You talk to her, Brian,' I remember her saying to me that day. 'You can't go playing about with names like that, it's wrong. Ellen will be so hurt.' Ellen was the name of an old friend of my mother's from domestic service days; it was the name of her own that Barbara loathed most of all.

'I think it's super to be able to choose one's own names,' I said. 'I don't care what I'm called, I won't change mine, Mum, but it's a good thing to be able to do what you want to.'

'Oh, you would take her side, Brian! Your father would do just the same.' My mother's small face seemed to get even smaller, and she started stroking the back of her left hand restlessly with the fingertips of the other. Her mouth curved down, and her whole presence seemed edgy and lacklustre, except for her brown eyes, which were shining only because they were moist. Not for the first time in my life, I regretted my mild assertion of a reasonably spirited point of view, and put my hand on the top of her stroking hand and held it.

'I'll talk to her. I don't know, I don't think it really matters, Mum, but I'll try and stop her doing anything silly.'

My mother's demeanour didn't change—it was always slow to—and I thought, then, about my father. He'd been glad to go at the end of his last leave, I could tell; and I knew my mother could tell, too. Most of the time, his existence didn't enter my head. I was absorbed in so many contradictory activities and speculations, at fifteen, that home and what went on there were just like the air or the weather to me, circumstances you lived in to which it wasn't worth giving a thought more than necessary. I was thinking about God and duty, I was out in the country half the time trying to see foxes, I served at Communion once a month, I was concluding that Christianity was rubbish because it made no provision for the idea of beauty, I was thinking about a film star called Gloria de Haven, I was acting the second witch in *Macbeth*, I was preaching the socialism of Bernard Shaw, I was spending break every morning exchanging ingenious insults with a boy who's now a professor of chemistry as we stood in a queue of boys waiting to buy half bun-rounds at the baker's. But when I did think of my father, it was always, now, about saying goodbye to him when he went back from his last leave.

That had been just over a year ago, in March 1942. He'd gone in the evening, wearing his civilian clothes—he'd said he'd just slip away after kissing us goodbye; we weren't even to come to the door with him. My mother had held his upper arms, her brown eyes wet—I saw how loth she was to display too much feeling, for fear of seeing some trace of impatience in him. My sister had jumped up and made him catch her, as we'd done when we were smaller; she burst into tears, with her head on his shoulder.

'There, Nan,' he said. 'You'll like your new school. And the war won't be long now.'

None of us believed that. We never doubted we'd win; but the fighting in north Africa didn't seem to bring the great day very much nearer. As my father went out of the sitting-room door, I went with him, and out into the front garden. In spite of what he'd said, he didn't make me go back. We lived on a new housing estate, all bungalows, all behind high privet hedges. It was silent in the darkness out there, but it was a starry night, and I could see his glasses shining as he turned to me at the gate. I threw my arms round him, and he murmured,

'Look after your mother, old man.' Then he gripped me very tight by the shoulders and shook me—almost trembling, it seemed to me. I heard him whisper sharply, 'Poor chap! poor chap!' Then he let go of me, and was off down the road without another word. I started to shout out to him, but stopped myself. It was three or four minutes before his footsteps were lost in the only other sound, the wind in the garden trees.

I was still thinking about that night as my mother and I sat in silence over the tea-things. Then the front door slammed, the sitting-room door opened and Barbara burst in, still in her beret and coat.

'I've done it!' she said.

My mother's look changed from vexation to alarm. 'What have you done?'

'Oh, nothing, Mum—I've just fixed it up, that's all. I'm going to have a private baptism after Evensong the third Sunday in April. You've got to come but I can say my names myself, it's definite.'

'You're not baptised to have names,' I said. 'You're baptised to make promises.'

'Oh, I know all about that,' my sister snapped at me. 'I know as much as you, stuck-up.'

'All right, all right,' I said. 'I just wanted to make sure.'

'What about the names?' my mother said.

'I'm going to change them. They'll still be the same on my birth certificate; you can go by that, Mum, I'll go by my baptism.'

'Oh, Barbara!' And my mother started to cry again.

The next few weeks, as far as she and Barbara were

concerned, were weeks of negotiation. Barbara was quite determined not to throw her chance away; but she agreed, after much angry talk, that she would keep 'Barbara' as a second name. However, 'Elizabeth' and 'Ellen' were right out. For her first name, she kept proposing candidates, but more to herself than to my mother. 'Juliet', I remember, was one that my mother rather desperately encouraged, since Barbara's birthday was at the end of July, and that seemed to make some sense of it. From time to time, my mother would throw the whole discussion over, and simply repeat, 'You can't change your names, it's just . . . ', then break into tears; but each time the outburst seemed less convincing. Finally, about a week before the baptism, my sister said, in a rather cheerful, unembittered way that sounded more like her usual self, 'All right, Mum, let's settle for Roberta Barbara. It sounds a bit woppy but I like it.' 'Roberta' had been one that my mother had paused over, because of a boy she'd known in the First World War called Robert, before she knew my father.

As for my father himself, we all knew he wouldn't mind what Barbara did. (And sure enough, a few days after the baptism, she had a letter from him beginning, 'Dear April, Veronica, Roberta, Theda, you'll always be the same old Nan to me'.) Anyway, 'Roberta Barbara' was agreed on, though not without my mother saying every day afterwards, 'Now you'll stick to it, won't you, Barbara? I've only agreed because that's what you've said.'

'Oh, don't keep going on about it,' was Barbara's usual reply to this.

I think the week before the baptism was the one in which we were doing a run-through of School Cert, a rehearsal for the real thing in the summer. I was busy with that; I was also out a lot those April evenings trying to see foxes, often taking my books with me and lying, reading, where I knew they might cross a field. We were only thirty miles from London, but because of the war foxes were common round us. It was the same for me, in a way, as for the foxes: London hardly impinged on my life, because since the war began my sister and I had never been allowed to go there. In any event, I took virtually no part in the debates going on between my mother and Barbara, in spite of what I'd promised my mother. Yet I was conscious of her distress, and often looked at her anxiously without saying anything. Clumsiness, loneliness, seemed to be encroaching on her day by day, but I was too self-absorbed, or simply too much in a child's relationship to her still, to do anything except notice. One night, however, I heard her crying quietly in her bedroom, a damp, poorly furnished, green-distempered room from which all trace of my father seemed to have gone, except for a few musty clothes at the dark end of the wardrobe rail. I went in and sat by her on the cold, puffy eiderdown, and she looked sharply at me through her tears.

'You don't help, Brian,' she said. 'Your father's away and he's on Barbara's side—he'd never help me with you anyway. And you don't help, you're always out.'

'Whatever can I do, Mum?' I said. But I put my arm round her, and she let it rest there.

Suddenly she responded to my gesture. 'Oh, I don't

know, it's all right, Brian,' she said. 'I know we've all got our little cross to bear in the war.' She wiped her eyes and forced herself to smile, and I thought how simple her needs really were—I remembered when we were smaller children, and to our eyes, at any rate, the family atmosphere was happy; she would sit evening after evening on a cut-down stool by the fire, knitting, and singing chapel hymns in a small but rather sweet voice, smiling as she remembered singing them with her two sisters in First World War congregations.

> Shall we gather at the river,
> The beautiful, the beautiful, the river?

She'd sing that one often, with a military swing, nodding her head forwards and sideways on each strong beat, pronouncing the words clearly like a teacher. But now her face was lined and colourless, and her chin drooped, as she sat on the bed beside me.

'Don't worry, Mum,' I said. 'Go to bed, it's going to be a lovely day tomorrow, it was a terrifically red sunset over the wood.' I had the sense not to say anything encouraging about my father. But as I went out of the bedroom, I noticed my own face in the wardrobe mirror—and that, too, had a long, solemn look on it that I'd never seen before.

So Barbara's day came. I don't think my mother had been to church since my father was called up, though before that we had often gone as a family to Evensong. My mother got out a buttercup-coloured suit with a matching bonnet, probably sold for sixteen-year-olds, but fitting her quite well, and of course much cheaper than something similar aimed at her own age. It was a sunny April day, with the leaves all coming out, and she looked quite dainty in it as we walked down to the church at quarter past six. My sister had a new cream-coloured woollen dress with brown facings—I think she wanted to look vaguely baptismal, but not too assertively so. I'd put on my usual grey suit. One or two neighbours had wanted to come, but my mother—still nervous, no doubt, about the whole thing—had told them it was just a family affair. However, Evelyn was coming; and another girl my sister liked, called Jeanette, who had been confirmed last year, was going to be her god-mother. I'd been disconcerted to hear this. Jeanette was tall, oval-eyed, with long legs which she would fling rather freely over the arms of armchairs. I wanted to curl up in those armchairs with her. But she scarcely noticed me, and never stayed in our house for very long. She was always on her way to a dance, the Guides, or some other energy-consuming activity.

When we went into the church, by the side door, we saw the two sitting in a pew halfway down the church, Evelyn in a pink costume and pink pancake hat, Jeanette in a white blouse and blue skirt. Like Barbara, Jeanette had no hat. They must have kept glancing over their shoulders, because they saw us at once and smiled. We joined them in the pew, Barbara next to them, then my mother, and me on the outside. As usual, there were only about twenty people in church; the organist, an old lady who lived in the village, was playing some drowsy, reverential music, not forgetting herself tonight and breaking into 'I'll Walk Beside You', as she had sometimes been known to do.

She struck up louder as the vicar and half the choir came out of the vestry door—the choir was only a couple of young women and two boys, and the women, who wore no surplices, were already seated in the choir-stalls. I liked the vicar, Mr Nettlebeck, whom I knew from serving, but he was an old man, completely absorbed in theological studies, who hardly distinguished one parishioner from another.

The service seemed to go slowly—we were all keyed up for what was going to follow it. But eventually the vicar and choir filed out again, the women in the procession this time. We sat where we were till the church was empty. Then we went to the font at the back of the church. Someone had put a vase of bluebells on the rim.

'I hope he doesn't send it flying,' said Evelyn, and she and Jeanette giggled.

'You'd have to call yourself "Bluebell", then, Roberta,' said Jeanette, and this time Barbara bit her lip to stop herself smiling.

My mother, I could see, was rather in awe of the occasion, and didn't want to say anything that might upset Barbara now. She sat down on a nearby pew, her hands folded in her lap, while I looked for the page in the prayer-book and told them the number.

Three or four minutes passed, and there was still no sign of Mr Nettlebeck. 'He's forgotten,' said Barbara, angrily.

I was suddenly afraid he had. 'I'll go and see,' I said— I had a sort of natural right of entry to the vestry from being a server. The sun was shining through the west window, and my long shadow went before me up the aisle.

I found the vicar in the vestry, alone, in his suit, bending over, putting on his bicycle-clips.

'Why, hello, Colin,' he said, 'what. . . .' His face fell. 'Oh my goodness gracious!' He reached down again for the cycle-clip that was already on one leg. 'Just coming, Colin. Tell them I won't be a minute.'

'All right, sir,' I said. I nodded as soon as I came out of the vestry door. My mother was standing up again by now. When I got to the font, Barbara said, 'He'd forgotten, hadn't he?' But this time, far from being angry, she was elated. I was suddenly afraid. She was planning something, and she felt the initiative in her hands now that the vicar had forgotten.

'Of course not,' I said. But she could tell I was lying. 'He's just coming,' I said to my mother, taking her lightly by the arm.

A moment later he came out and hurried down the aisle to us.

'Ah, how are you, Mrs Cotton?' he said to my mother, smiling, shaking her hand in both of his. 'And the baby?' he said, turning to my sister. 'Ah-ha! It's never too late, is it? And the godmother?'

'That's me,' said Jeanette, her big, oval eyes shining.

'Good! good! It's never too early, either!'

He removed the bluebells, and replaced them with a jug of water that was standing at the foot of the font, out of which he poured a little into the basin. Then he arranged us in front of him, my sister in the middle, my mother and me on the left, Jeanette and Evelyn on her right.

'Dearly beloved,' he began, 'forasmuch as all men are conceived and born in sin. . . . ' My mother was looking very calm and happy. Barbara seemed to have her teeth pressed rather tight together. When we came to the first prayer, it appeared we were going to stand where we were, just bowing our heads. Mr Nettlebeck was growing more lyrical, his voice rising: ' . . . Wash her and sanctify her with the Holy Ghost'—he seemed to love that pairing of verbs—'that she, being delivered from Thy wrath, may be received into the ark of Christ's Church. . . .' We were getting near to Barbara's part in the ceremony. 'Well-beloved,' he said, looking at her, ' . . . dost thou renounce the Devil and all his works, the vain pomp and glory of the world. . . ?' My spirits rose at this phrase. The glory of the world's got nothing to do with the Devil, I thought. If the Church thinks that, the Church must be wrong. I was thinking of the sun going down in amazing streaks of pink over the wood behind our house, and a fox hurrying across the field, its fur almost crimson in the sunset.

Barbara's voice rang out, high-pitched but clear. 'I renounce them all.'

'Wilt thou then obediently keep God's holy will and commandments, and walk in the same all the days of thy life?'

'I will endeavour to do so,' Barbara said sharply, 'God being my helper.'

We prayed, and suddenly we were there. Mr Nettlebeck took Barbara's right hand, and said softly, 'What is your name?'

'Scarlett Blanche,' Barbara replied without hesitation.

Evelyn let out a screech. My mother bit back a cry. I felt the blood drain from my face. Mr Nettlebeck noticed nothing. Barbara was standing absolutely still, with her hand in his; she was looking straight at the church wall, and I could see a smile on the corner of her lips. I took my mother's arm; I could feel her body shaking with sobs now. I hardly took in the making of the cross, but I did see Mr Nettlebeck smile as he said, 'Seeing now, dearly beloved brethren, that this person is regenerate and grafted into the body of Christ's Church. . . .'

In a moment, he was shaking hands with us all and saying goodbye. The moment he turned his back, Barbara headed for the church door. The other girls looked awkwardly at us, then followed her without a word, obviously not knowing what to say. As she opened the heavy door, Barbara turned and said, 'Sorry, Mum.' The moment they were all outside, the girls ran. I could hear their footsteps clattering through the churchyard, then Jeanette's loud laugh.

I helped my mother out of the church. She was crying openly now. I could see the girls still, at the far end of the churchyard, between the cypress trees, their pale legs flashing in the evening sun. And as I put my arm round my mother, I began to feel emotions I had never known before. I hated Barbara, and I hated my father. It seemed to me she was running towards him, far away in north Africa, and my father was lifting her up and swinging her round and dancing with her. 'Poor chap,' I could hear him saying. And as I squeezed my mother's shoulder, I hated her as much as I grieved for her, weeping and sniffing there, wanting to rage at Barbara—I could feel it—but not able to bring herself even to do that. And accompanying all this hatred, I felt a strange fear. My sense of freedom was fading: far into the future I could see myself with my arm going round a weak, complaining woman, while the legs of a girl I longed to be with twinkled out of sight beneath dark, distant trees.

Bert 'n' Shirl

RUDOLF NASSAUER

AS SOON as Bert was properly awake he followed a certain routine. First he put his hand down his pyjama trousers to feel his scrotum. Nowadays he liked to scratch this tegument, and he'd long overcome any shyness in front of Shirl, who knew exactly what he was up to. She actually companioned his scratching by playfully pulling taut the skin beneath her bosoms and at times that on the inside of her thighs. In those areas the skin had become slack, there were ripples and unfortunate folds, and to tauten herself up for a few moments gave her the illusion of younger days. Not that she minded ageing herself, but she had been repelled for a time by Bert's ageing. He'd grown far too heavy, it had sapped his energy. It was a job for him to keep awake after half past nine at night. Now and again they went to a film during the day. He'd grown idle, too idle even to hold a book in his hands, let alone to read it.

But then, don't forget, there is pleasure in giving in. Gradually, having failed to goad Bert into renewed activity, Shirl had condoned his sluggishness and allowed uncaring to seep into her fastidiousness. Every week a lady came to the house to do her nails (Bert's as well), but when it came to choosing the colour of the varnish she left this to the manicurist. Same with her clothes. As far as the shop assistants who helped dress her were concerned, Shirl was a customer to earn commission on. Everything they sold her was expensive, but she looked removed from her clothes, remote from the effect of colour and cut of any of her garments, inelegant and drab.

Bert lay on Shirl's right. He fumbled about with his left hand. After a few strokes of her rib-cage and one or two forays to her legs (without coming closer he couldn't really stretch far enough for what he was trying to get at), they ended up every morning holding hands. A moment after finding her hand, Bert's right hand was on the knob of the intercom which connected him to Alfonso and Teresa, the Spanish couple, in the kitchen. First he asked Shirl: 'You want a little soup this morning, dear? A little bouillon?'

'Just a drop.'

'With an egg in it?'

'No thanks, dear.'

'Have an egg in it, Shirl. It's good for you.'

'Gives me indigestion.'

'No. Perhaps you'd better not. Alfonso! Oh, excuse me, dear—good morning Alfonso, hold on—I thought I'd got rid of my wind.'

'That's all right, dear. You're with friends.'

'I *am* sorry.—Alfonso, could you bring us some soup? The consommé, just a small amount. Bring the tureen up and a couple of cups, and put two raw eggs in one of the cups. I'll pour the soup on up here, else if you do it in the kitchen, by the time Teresa's brought it up the eggs'll be hard. You understand?'

Some amusing noise came out of the loudspeaker.

There must have been a loose connection, because loud crackling mingled with Alfonso's Spanish sibilance.

'What's he farting about?' Shirl asked.

'He'd asking what else we'd like.'

'Tell him to bring the fucking soup. I'm starving!'

'Alfonso, can you still hear me?'

'Yeth, Signor Bert.'

'Bring up the soup and then we'll tell you what else we'd like.'

'And ask Teresa to get off her fanny and bring the papers.'

'Is Teresa there, Alfonso? Ask her to be so kind as to bring up the papers right away. Thank you.'

Now and again Bert still managed an erection, but it was at such irregular intervals and at times so unexpected that Shirl was never around to be fucked. Bert didn't give it too much thought, but when he did think about it he found some of the sources of his excitement so astonishing that he didn't really believe it had anything to do with him, and that if he stood up suddenly it was merely a fluke, or some weird chemical process in his balls. He didn't know much about sex, though he'd not been at all averse to it in his time. But for two or three years now cracks had appeared in his desire, obesity had made parts of his body insensitive, his biceps ached if he had to support himself on his arms for any length of time. (At the health farm three months ago he hadn't managed even one press-up.) Besides, he felt, succumb! So his penis didn't rise up first thing in the morning as it used to, regularly. Perhaps, though, it might again. Sex goes in cycles. Until he was six or seven, or was it four or eleven (he'd forgotten and who was there to ask about such things?), nothing had happened down there. Then it had. So it might again. Perhaps it had to do with the bladder. As soon as he woke up he wanted to pee quite urgently, but always after he'd peed his penis shrivelled up even more. It was awful! Every morning, therefore, he tried to prolong the time of holding back, vaguely hoping for a miracle, for his copulatory organ to become once more fat, hard and upstanding, until holding back was a pleasant pain, a gamble of body and mind, both nice to play with if both are yours. Shirl did the same. Some time ago they'd discussed it. They actually thought of each other, that's after all what counts, Bert had said.

'Isn't that right, Shirl?' he'd asked.

'Oh, get stuffed, you silly old fart!' (He'd interrupted her reading the *Financial Times.*)

Thus—in quite unhealthy fashion, some doctors would say—they competed with each other every morning as to who could hold back his or her water longest. No advantage was gained by either one of them winning the race, as there were two bathrooms *en suite,* each one with a toilet.

'Thanks, Teresa,' Shirl said. Teresa had set the cups and the steaming bowl of soup on the trolley and had pushed it over to Shirl's side of the bed. Bert smiled. The trolley reminded him of a lovely puffer-train.

'Did you bring any bread?' Bert asked Teresa.

'No,' she said, staccato.

'You don't need any bloody bread, dear. Control yourself.'

'Just a slice of the black rye, Teresa, d'you mind?'

'Righway.'

'Or make it two, dear. And bring the trolley round to my side. I'll serve. Thank you.'

'Teresa,' Shirl called out, 'before you go down pass me my dressing-gown. Thanks. The pink one, yes.'

Teresa did as Shirl had asked, then looked at Bert whilst pointing at Shirl's dressing-gown. Bert nodded. She passed him his blue one which was hanging over the back of his chair, just out of his reach. With adroit dexterity they slung their respective dressing-gowns over their shoulders.

'I think I'd like a few mushrooms before the fish this morning. How 'bout you, dear?' Bert asked. 'There're field mushrooms at present. Very good.'

'Yeah, why not? Tell Alfonso to sprinkle plenty of parsley on mine.'

'And then haddock, I think. Or would you rather have a kipper?'

'Haddock.'

Bert gave the order. The soup was quite delicious.

'Did you know, Shirl, Toscanini had consommé every morning of his life? Practically lived on it.'

'What you conducting tonight? Another trombone concert?'

There was a veneer of anger on Bert's face. Shirl sensed it, looked at him and smiled.

'Sorry, darling. Did he really?'

'Yeah.'

A moment later she was once more immersed in the pages of the *FT*. He had picked up *The Times*.

'Good old Imps!' Shirl said.

'Oh dear! Tony Sands's died,' Bert told her on this occasion. Conversation was not always as lively as this, or as pleasant. Shares dropped to 'fuck' and 'shit', and most days Bert knew no one mentioned in the obituary column. As soon as someone made death Bert and Shirl became familiar with them.

'Poor old Tony. What'd he croak from? Does it say?'

'No. Died three days ago—yes, the seventeenth.'

'Poor sod. Couldn't make the eighteenth! He was a nice guy,' Shirl said.

'At Mortlake.'

'That's where his wife lived. Must have gone home to die.'

'Were they divorced?'

'Thought he'd left her. Hadn't he?'

'Didn't we meet her once down at Richmond?'

'That was Stella. He called her his Thames-side folly. He was very funny.'

'Thames-side folly!' Bert chortled.

'Probably fucked himself to death.'

Bert's hunger was stronger than his stamina to read. He hadn't actually intended to have more than one cup of soup, but he put the paper down to ladle out another cupful. He'd forced himself to leave half a piece of the black bread on his plate but knew whilst he was doing so that his resistance to breaking his resolve was unreliable. It was much like giving a lettuce leaf to one rabbit to take to another. He simply could not control his overwhelming desire.

'Some more soup, Shirl? Let me give you a drop more.'

'No more, thanks. Mushrooms coming.'

Shirl had marvellous ears. She could hear the phone even when they were sitting in the garden. Bert used the pool in the summer, though as seldom as possible. It's terrible to get wet if you prefer not to. He enjoyed confusing staying afloat with keeping fit. That's why now and again he immersed himself in the pool, and with one or two strokes swam a length.

Teresa knocked and brought the mushrooms. Shirl at once stuck her fork into one, one she'd held in position with thumb and forefinger, and ate it.

'Hm!' she said, licking her fingers, 'tell Alfonso, Teresa, the mushrooms are lovely.'

'Would you like a little. . . . Teresa, wait a moment, please,' Bert said. 'Would you like a little white wine with them? That really brings out the flavour. A little Mosel. Teresa, bring up. . . . '

'Not for me, dear.'

'Teresa, bring up the bottle of Mosel, the Serriger, it's that long green bottle, there's some left from last night. We had it with the lobster. And a couple of glasses, if you please.'

'You're incorrigible.'

'What the hell? Stanton drank a bottle of champagne every morning for breakfast, by himself. When he had a guest the guest had another.'

'No need to copy bad habits. What did it do for Stanton? Killed the fucker,' Shirl quipped, the smooth surface of the mushrooms and their oily texture in no way impeding her speech as she spoke with her mouth full.

'Come on, dear. Wasn't the champagne killed Stanton

Gould, but his ride as Chancellor of the Exchequer. He worked a sixteen-hour day, some days eighteen. That's what killed him.'

'Hard work's never killed anyone.'

'Balls!'

'Not that you'd know what I'm talking about,' Shirl said, finding Bert's hand and slapping it affectionately. To retaliate, he dropped his fork and tried hitting her arm, laughing.

'What time is it, dear?' he asked.

'Half past.'

'I said I'd ring Hirschel at eleven at the hotel. Shall we see them tonight, or'd you rather leave it over till tomorrow?'

'Tonight's fine. I'm having my hair done at four.'

'I'll arrange things. And dear, don't, please, call Stanton a fucker. With him I don't like it. Turns my stomach.'

'That's good exercise.'

Bert couldn't help being amused by Shirl's cheek, but as far as Stanton Gould was concerned he did feel a bit uneasy when she lashed out at him. It was to write a book on Gould that Bert had come over from the States in '47, and for two years he'd been more in than out of No. 11 Downing Street, copying stuff and taking notes, and observing the Chancellor, who had taken quite a liking to Bert. He'd met Shirl about that time, but he hadn't seen too much of her, as she was busy making a fortune in toys, and four years ago now—they married in '50—the family firm had been bought by an American concern, leaving Shirl rich. Thus talents cross-fertilise, nation to nation.

When the fish course arrived Teresa looked different. Bert noticed her cheeks were redder. She'd put some rouge on, it made her brown eyes more sparkling, she looked charming, particularly her two thumbs as she turned the plate on Bert's tray to make the fish face the right way. Bert had time to touch one of her thumbs, very gently. It made her blush.

'Thank you, Teresa. I'll have my eggs scrambled this morning. And you, Shirl?'

'Fried.'

Teresa wiped her brow with her white apron—not, as Shirl remarked once she'd left the room, the most appetising of gestures.

'It's the stairs,' Bert said in Teresa's defence.

'Quite. Perhaps we ought to sleep in the fucking kitchen. That'd save her legs.'

Bert admired activity from afar but himself could not cope with it. Never had been able to. His legs and feet weren't built to walk fast, and no doubt this had had a profound influence on his growth, physical and mental. The highlights of his day—sometimes in fact it took two or three days before there was something which lit him up for a second or two—were like streaks women have dyed into their hair, which have to be frequently redone to stop them fading out. History. It had to do with having or not having a history. Not a sense of it, a feel for it, not, as they'd taught him at school, 'the feeling of ratio which history teaches you'. That's the phrase Stubbs had used, who'd taught history at middle school. Bert had never understood what it meant, and didn't now—only vaguely. That was the trouble. Everything in his brain, every mental picture he tried to construct, was built on a foundation of sand. Sometimes—it had been truer still a few years ago when his brain had been more agile—he'd been able to juggle ideas about quite nicely, to build fairly tall mental structures, sometimes with a bullying kind of humour. By that technique he'd warded off argument; it had allowed him to perform without destructive interruption. Even Shirl had at times listened to him admiringly, without, as she did now, blistering everything he said with gibes, giving him to understand that she was fond of him although he talked a load of shit.

When Teresa brought the eggs, Bert suggested to Shirl that a few slices of glazed tongue (cut fairly thick, otherwise it's tasteless, he'd implored Teresa to tell Alfonso) would go nicely with the remainder of the Serriger.

'There's only a drop left, hardly a glass each, it'd be a waste not to drink it. It won't go with the eggs.'

'Fine! I like tongue.'

'Teresa, have we any croissants?'

'Yeth.'

'Then do bring a few up with the toast and the marmalade. And a plate of tongue. Thank you.'

There's nobody you hear of nowadays can trace his family back to before the Norman Conquest. That's how Bert had figured it out years ago. He'd written a dull book on Stanton Gould. He wasn't an historian, or a biographer. Stanton's life hadn't helped. He'd been a dry old stick, abstemious, a bit of an aesthete, a touch precious, a do-gooder able to afford doing good. With money and lineage you can do most things. With money alone, nothing. That's what Bert was getting at. God! It was complicated to have an original thought. Would it ever be possible? Was he starting another depression? You know how he would tell? The curves of his top lip went stiff. It felt like stiffeners they put into collars having been shoved in above his lips. It put him off speaking, made him quiet. At best everything he said sounded sad. And that in turn. . . . That's why he'd first started to grow a beard. When you're sad it doesn't show up so much.

By a quarter to, Shirl had done her sums. She'd pencilled a few figures on the pad, and now dialled Mr Hanbury. Hers was always the first call Mr Hanbury took. He needed three quarters of an hour in the office to work things out.

'Sell Carters. They're boring. Haven't moved for months. Not really. Duples have. Sell those as well, I reckon I'll show about four thousand profit on them. Sell them, and put an order in when they're twenty pence down. They're bound to drop again.'

Within a few minutes the deals were done. Somehow, Bert felt, though he always listened with fascination, there was something crude in the association of money and lying in bed. Money should be made out of bed, by people who are dressed. The idea of nude shop assistants made him smile. That proved to him he wasn't heading for a depression.

Shirl got up. Bert as well—though he waited, as every day, a moment longer. Quite unbeknown to Shirl because she took no notice of it, he was going to hold his water a few seconds longer than her.

That there was nobody nowadays could trace his family to before the Norman Conquest, was that true? Bert, anyhow, couldn't think of anyone. It struck him as quite a nice idea that we all have an equally long lineage. Bert was going to come back to this later on, it was a vague and interesting enough idea for him to spend a bit of time ruminating on, when he was less occupied with other things. He was holding his penis an inordinately long time to drain it of the last drop of urine. Having held back so long there was certainly a small ration of pleasure he had earned, though it was quickly spent. That's why he held on, squeezing himself and running his hand over his organ as if it were the nipple of an udder, until he was completely dry. He'd not yet had his toast and marmalade, and now climbed back into bed to have it. So did Shirl.

Shirl was more lucky with filling her mind with employment. She was obsessed with money and therefore never had to wait for something to catch her fancy which would occupy her for a minute or so. She was good with money, loved making it, had a curious deep-rooted respect for it, all of which made her cautious not to waste it, to lose it or be careless with it.

No matter how much money Shirl had made—and her fortune had increased vastly over the last twenty years—she suffered dreadfully on account of an excellent memory, particularly when it came to debts. Whenever her mind was unoccupied for a moment, the picture of some debtor prancing about, going to a restaurant instead of eating a bag of chips, looking after his wife and

mistress instead of repaying what he owed her, hurt
Shirl so much that it forced her to shower abuse on
whatever she was doing, sometimes on whoever she was
with. Up it would come again, twenty years later—she'd
suddenly swear about a boyfriend she'd had twenty years
ago who'd not had enough money to take her out to a
good meal so she had paid, as well as buying him a suit
and shirts and tie so that decent restaurants would let
him in. And when they'd gone off to Paris she'd paid,
and to Wales. Of course the fucking sod owed it to her,
what made anyone think he didn't? He'd done some
broadcasts and written some articles, he was working
on Welsh TV now, she kept track of him, wrote him the
odd letter now and again to remind him of his debt—curt,
tough, abusive reminders that she was still around and, if
he was such a big shit as not to pay up, she could at least
try to keep his conscience guilty.

'Oh, would you mind, Shirl, dear, if Edna did you first
this morning? I'd quite forgotten she comes early this
week and I arranged to ring Hirschel at eleven.'

'I'd prefer it, 'cause I'm meeting Sylvia for lunch. Got
trouble again with that prick of a husband. Wants to
bugger her and she won't let him,' Shirl was laughing.
'Apparently he screams the place down every night.'

'You do make up stories, Shirl. It's not fair, you know.
I like Bob. Ask them over. They haven't been here for
ages.'

'He's a pain in the arse. Always on about his bloody
boat. Wish he'd drown.'

'And she's sweet.'

'I like her.'

Edna came to the house every day to massage Bert and Shirl. She was short and fat, tough as a monkey. She'd come from Cape Town, leaving a husband behind, a political prisoner. On good days she told marvellous stories which made her clients jump with laughter. On bad days she relieved her anguish by kneading them so hard they changed colour. Her equipment was a folding canvas table on which her clients laid their weary flesh. Shrieks of laughter came from Shirl's dressing-room as Bert called Hirschel at Claridges.

Hirschel took a long time answering. Was he in the bathroom? Teresa was clearing the breakfast away.

'Bring me, Teresa, please, some fresh orange juice. About three or four of the Jaffas . . . hallo? Hallo. . . ? Yes, about three or four of the Jaffas pressed. The fish's made me thirsty. Hallo? Hallo?'

It was unlike Hirschel to have forgotten that Bert had arranged to ring at eleven. Punctilious to the letter, yesterday a man who'd survived the holocaust of the Jews in Europe, today head of a world-wide financial empire, why the hell didn't he answer his phone? It *was* today he'd arranged to ring him—that's right, they'd spoken together yesterday afternoon shortly after Hirschel had flown in from New York.

'No reply from 406 and 7.'

'I'll ring later.'

No point leaving a message. In a few minutes Hirschel would ring off his own bat. Some good reason must have kept him from the phone. Bert thought: 'The best brains have streaks of originality and therefore are capable of surprising you.' What excuse would Hirschel give?

Hirschel hadn't rung by the time it was Bert's turn for massage. Edna set up her contraption in his dressing-room and he mounted it to have himself touched more or less all over. He always started by closing his eyes and, egged on by Edna's magic grip, he saw himself a sprinter, a Pele of the Western world. Edna, though, didn't like dreamy clients.

'Is like messing about with a corpse with your eyes closed,' she'd say, and if he was slow enough not to open them at once and wide she'd give him a poke in the ribs or some other ticklish part.

'Who knows what you're thinking about with your eyes shut? All of a sudden you might come and I get accused of having it off with you.'

'I'd like that,' Bert said.

Edna was nice about it. 'Get away with you. You're what they call a.m. randy.' She told him to turn over.

At one time, to watch Shirl dress in the morning, or just to think of her doing so, made him randy as hell. Now, whilst Edna poured oil on his body, he shuddered at the cruelty of the thought of Shirl dressing not to evoke his lust but to camouflage her tired body.

Hirschel hadn't rung by the time Shirl was leaving, nor could Bert get any new information from reception when he rang the hotel.

'I'll be back by six, so get Hirschel to come over for a drink so I can have a bath and change before we go out. Book a table.'

'Where? Where'd you like to eat?'

'I'll leave it to you, OK? Not Chinese though, or Jap stuff. The Capitol'd be fun. Rack of lamb. Try. I'm late.'

For the first time that day Shirl left the bedroom. She brushed her shoe against the Giacometti statuette they used for a door-stopper, cursed and gave it a bit of a kick so that it fell over and back a few inches. Downstairs she opened the breakfast-room door, called out, 'Good morning,' to Alfonso in the kitchen and gave one or two instructions to Teresa before leaving for the day.

Bert was a slow dresser. He had a large wardrobe to choose from and most days tried on several shirts and trousers, socks even, before coming to his final choice of the day, which always ended up being less eccentric than he'd wished—conventional, even, as far as his face and figure allowed. At eighteen stone pushing nineteen, there're all kinds of things you can't wear without looking ridiculous, some of which, like pin- or chalk-stripes, are the height of convention. Nor did Bert look very pleasing in casual clothes, open collars and blazers. Fat people must wear ties to give the simulation of being held together and breaking the flow downwards of their bulging flesh. It took some time every day for Bert to get used to what he was wearing. He rang Hirschel again. Still no reply. Reception told him to call back at two.

This time when he put the phone down Bert felt a taut feeling in his stomach. His heartbeat was fast. There'd been something too firm and officious in the receptionist's voice, something a touch commanding which filled him with unease. That feeling increased as he went downstairs to his study. He asked Teresa for a pot of tea and some sweet biscuits. Probably he'd not eat lunch. He'd decide later on.

He had nothing to do. He'd not done any work since his book on Stanton Gould twenty years ago, except for two articles for his old college magazine which he still picked up and glanced at now and again. He liked fingering his past efforts just to show himself he was capable, if he set his mind to it, of serious work. The walls were lined with books. There were stacks of photographs, magazines and large unopened envelopes, letters were strewn on tables and chairs, catalogues, brochures and wine merchants' lists lay on the lower shelves. Bert always kept the door of his study ajar, and when he wasn't actually in the room the door was kept open just wide enough for the few guests who came to the house to catch a glimpse of intellectual endeavour.

As we get older everything becomes history. The scar where we cut ourselves on a sharp stone, where our sister pricked us with her pen, where they lanced an abscess, it's changed little but become more of us, flesh-fossil in our flesh. Bert at one time had reflected how he'd become used to doing nothing, how this had started when his interest in Stanton had waned after Stanton's death, how he'd gladly become a mourner in the most romantic fashion, which was to deny himself the right to be active so as to share the inactivity of the dead. A most charming idea.

By now Bert's inactivity was an immutable part of his progress through each day. The chair at his desk was soft and comfortable and often as soon as he sat down he simply dozed off. Just before sinking into oblivion Bert took a look at the clock on his desk. Time to ring Hirschel? Two, she'd said, ring at two. A long time to wait. Over two hours. He'd have a short kip, then order lunch.

Bert really felt rested after half an hour's sleep. Was that all he'd slept? The masseur who worked at Danieli's in Venice always told his clients to have a relaxed sleep after he'd worked on them. It worked. Bert had woken up refreshed, ready to tackle anything. Monday and Tuesday, he decided, he'd go to the States to see his dad. Why not? Shirl wouldn't want to come. Perhaps they'd meet in Paris on Wednesday. He'd book a table at L'Archestrate and they'd have fresh duck pâté foie gras with sliced truffles and sea bass in red wine sauce. In New York he'd eat dairy lunches and then move on elsewhere for pastrami sandwiches and relish. He would, if he could, eat all day long. Was there greater pleasure than satisfying taste-buds, anything as singular, intimate or varied?

Sight of the framed picture on his desk of the children sent a slight shock through him. Jeremy and Blanche. Blanche was in New York living with what Shirl called a gorilla, on account of his black beard and ever-open mouth. He'd lately, aged thirty-two, taken up music, guitar and banjo, the first time.

'No doubt he fucks Blanche adequately,' Bert had said to Shirl.

'Sure.'

Why, Bert didn't know, but Blanche disturbed him. Probably he wouldn't bother even to see her. He'd ring her from Kennedy airport on his way back and tell Shirl he hadn't managed to get hold of her. Last time they'd had a row. He could see some of his faults in her and couldn't stand it.

At five to two he'd finished his lunch and his hand was on the phone, but he didn't lift the receiver until two. This time reception put him straight through.

'Hirschel, you shyster, where you been?'

'Mr Levine's. . . . Who's that speaking?'

' "Who's that speaking", my arse! Stop bullshitting. I'm not one of your creditors! I rang you at eleven on the dot and been hanging around the phone ever since waiting for you to call back. It's Bert, who else?'

'Mr Levine. . . . '

Bert changed the receiver from his left hand to his right to free his left to scratch the small of his back over on that side. He got there. A nice feeling.

'Now listen,' Bert said when he held the receiver to his ear once more. 'Can you come over here by six and we go out from here, 'cause Shirl'll be back by then and we have a drink first?'

'Mr Hirschel Levine passed away this morning. I'm sorry to have to tell you this. You were obviously close friends.'

'Close friends? Who's that speaking? Stop fart-arsing about, Hirschel.'

'I'm afraid no one is playing about, sir. Mr Levine died about 10.30 this morning. I'm the assistant manager. We're contacting Mr Levine's family so that the body can, if so desired, be repatriated.'

'Yeah. You *are* serious. Now I can tell. I'm sorry I was joking about like this.'

'That's all right, sir.'

'But Mr Levine and I are old friends. Were. . . .' At

first the tense with the dead is a bit confusing.

'Would you by any chance know where we could contact Mrs Levine? There's no reply from the New York address.'

'She's in Paris with her sister. She's supposed to come in later today. I've got numbers, if you'd just wait a minute. It's no good ringing her now. Or perhaps you could try. They might just be back from lunch.'

Bert was good on addresses. They were neatly written down in the little wafer telephone book he always carried about with him.

'326 4752. Paris, of course. The code is. . . .'

'We have that, sir. Thank you.'

'What, can you tell me, Mr Levine, did he die of? He was fine. I spoke to him last night.'

'The doctors haven't reported yet. He's been taken to Paddington Green.'

'What's at Paddington Green? A cemetery?'

'St Mary's, Paddington Green. It's a hospital.'

'You don't give a guy a chance, do you? Why the hurry?'

'Policy, sir. Death is frightening to hotel guests.'

'You bet Hirschel was fucking frightened. Outlived Belsen and dies at Claridges! Bit of a joke. Suppose in the end it doesn't matter where you croak, does it?'

'No, sir. I don't suppose it does.'

Bert, trying to be as profound as he dared be with an assistant hotel manager he'd never met, realised he was getting cruder than he wanted to be.

'Gee! He was tough as a nut, Hirschel Levine. You know the sort of nut I mean? Walnuts with gnarled shells, the kind that keep all the year. To open them you have to press the cracker so hard that in the end you shatter the fucking kernel and you're left with nothing. And you've had him taken away I won't even have a chance to see him again. I hate hospitals, and I certainly won't go into a morgue. Fuck that! You see, the nut's cracked so much there's nothing left, if you see what I mean.'

'I'm sorry, sir, but you'll find all the top hotels in London have the same policy.'

'I dare say. So there's no point in coming over, is there? Perhaps you'd leave a message for Mrs Levine to call me as soon as she gets in. Bert, Bert Strauss. S-T-R-A-U-S-S, like in ostrich. That's what the name means. It's German for ostrich.'

How amusing Bert could be, how fluently he could state one fact and link it to another, provided he wasn't interrupted and had a ready listener. He liked the phone. He felt people were ear-bound the other end whilst he was speaking. They had to pay attention to what he was saying, to concentrate and not do other things, walk about, powder their nose, pee, eat, fart even (because that might be heard). It was like being plugged in and energised, and the moment the conversation was over the tap was turned off, the rubber ball of conversation lost its valve mid-air and splodged noisily to ground.

'I will leave a message that you've rung, sir.'

'Strauss. S-T-R-A-U-S-S. You got it right, have you?'

'I have, Mr Strauss. Thank you.'

'Who taught this fucking little squirt to say "Thank you" like that and put the phone down?' Bert sat there livid, shaking with anger. Rage, if he continued holding the phone in his fist, would ensue. The purring from the earpiece grew louder, the noise was an insult; he couldn't work out why as quick as he wanted to. A moment later he put his receiver down. There wasn't any point in holding on with no one the other end.

That's when it came home to Bert the first time, that Hirschel was dead. 'What the fuck! The son of a bitch won't be coming here this evening. Tough old Hirschel's stopped breathing, and now he's as dead as his Belsen mates.'

There was (had been) a funny thing about Hirschel. He never carried any dough on him, never enough to pay the restaurant bill, tip the cloakroom attendant. It'd often struck Bert as funny. They'd laughed about it, he and Shirl. Bert liked wads of notes; Hirschel, though, felt something unclean about money, that's what he'd once told them. 'You don't know who's touched it, whether they had clean hands or VD. That's also why I don't gamble. Can't get myself to touch the chips. Same reason.' Hirschel had strong views about the contagion of disease. In the camps he'd sometimes traded a scrap of food for a few drops of water to wash in. Once or twice Shirl had made cruel forays into alternative causes for Hirschel's cashlessness. 'I get a funny feeling at times Hirschel's Gauguin isn't paid for, nor the rest of his pictures, that he's borrowed on one and with the money paid for another, and so on.'

'Bet he's done himself in,' Shirl said when Bert told her what'd happened. He hadn't phoned her at the hairdresser—why should he have done? There was nothing

Shirl could do about it, there was no point in her knowing before she had to. Also, he wanted to be in on the
drama of telling her, seeing her reaction, her face, hearing
her expressions. Besides, Bert had discovered during the
afternoon, they weren't as close to Hirschel as they'd
thought. Sometimes it's hard to tell how close you are
to someone until the person is dead. Rella Levine must
have thought likewise about Bert and Shirl, because she
didn't ring the whole afternoon, and she was bound to
have arrived. The Levines were, after all, expert trav-
ellers and past masters at converging at precise hours in
particular places, no matter how far apart they'd started
off that morning. Mrs Levine just hadn't bothered to
ring.

'You're fucking mad, Shirl. I like your hair. It take
long?'

'Three hours of hell. Thank you, dear. Glad you like
it.'

'They whisked poor old Hirschel out of fucking
Claridges in a flash. Did you know they get rid of
corpses at the double so's not to frighten the hotel
guests?'

'I'm starving.'

'I'll call Teresa, dear. I had a long conversation with
one of the managers of the hotel, he told me that.
Quite a charming man he was. Teresa, bring us a plate
each of smoked salmon, thank you.'

'That'd be lovely,' Shirl said. 'And a drink.'

'There's some Krug on ice. Bring us a bottle of that.'

'Lovely!'

'And then—just wait a minute, Teresa—how 'bout

some hot asparagus? I always like something hot after champagne, it's the acidity in the wine. But don't let's spoil our appetite 'cause I booked at the Capitol at 7.30 to eight.'

'We'll have dinner just the two of us, eh! That'll make a lovely change, darling.'

'Yeah.'

They ate alone most nights. They believed in their love for each other, that their friends were numerous, and that their intellectual calibre was more than sufficient to see them happily through their part of the twentieth century. Somewhere all men and women have one craving which they satisfy to compensate all others. Bert and Shirl's eating was inspired.

The salmon and champagne were delicious. Bert and Shirl discussed the asparagus. The green ones were tougher but more tasty than the white ones blanched by the earth. They decided in future to have some of each, the one for taste, the other for texture. As Shirl bent low to put her mouth round the next asparagus—she couldn't hold back from sucking it in before she spoke—she said, 'Tony Sands and Hirschel Levine in one day, poor sods! Pass the pepper-mill, dear.'

Bert dunked some bread in the melted butter and blotted up as much of it as he could before putting the squashy mess in his mouth. For a moment they both looked at each other, amused and shameless at having been caught at a clumsy point of eating. Each of them looked a Picasso subject. Dressed, they looked bare, their mouths glistening with grease and smudged, she showing shiny patches on her powdered chin, he streaks

of varnish on his beard as if the paint had spilled over
and dried before correction. Bert wiped his mouth and
beard with the back of his hand.

'Yeah,' he said, 'poor fuckers! Still, Hirschel made it
to Claridges. A long way from fucking Belsen.'

Shirl got up and let one rip.

'I'm going to have a shit and a bath. Then we go and
eat, OK, darling?'

'Don't be too long, dear. I said 7.30 to eight.'

Shirl picked up a paper and went off. Bert went to see
Alfonso. He wanted to talk to him. He'd wanted to see
him all day but the news of Hirschel had upset his plans.
The haddock was fine but it needed to be a bit more
smoked and salty. Tell the fishmonger. Also, when you
brine the tongue don't soak it too long afterwards. Bert
liked it quite salty.

'I suppose it's age, Alfonso. Getting older. The taste-
buds here in your mouth, on your tongue'—he pointed
out—'get a bit tired and need stronger stuff. I've found—
isn't that interesting, Alfonso?—that as I've gotten older
I use much more salt than before.'

Alfonso smiled. He didn't understand. Teresa was
there. She'd translate for him later on what Signor Bert
had said. Alfonso found it too hard to understand Bert.
Bert used so many words, he read so many books, he
was very clever. He liked him very much, even though he
couldn't understand him, or hardly.

The Mountainy Man

CATHERINE ROCKS

I HAS the bastable in my hands tipping the soda cake on to the table when I sees them coming up the boreen. I drops it real quick and turns to my da. For I knows it's to make the match they're come—though I never did think it would happen this quick.

And he, seeing the way I am, comes up to the window and looks out. 'It's Joe Hayes,' he says quiet, and he watches them come up the boreen.

But I don't wait. I rushes out past the outhouses and into the cow-house, for the cows are in the fields at that time of the year, and it's dark and empty with only the smell of the cows left.

I can see the men out there in the yard, but they don't see me, being in the dark. Joe Metal Hayes—he was called Metal on account of his mean ways—is at the head, striding out like a turkey-cock on his short legs. And I sees his small little eyes under his foxy brows staring round like they always done, like he was looking for something all the time.

Behind him comes Phil the Fluter—we calls him that on account of he sung it the time Father Ryan put on the concert for the School Building Fund. And I knows he's to make the match, him being a second cousin.

I hears their boots on the cobbles as they comes into

the yard past the haggart and it's like I am in a dream, and it can't be happening.

And then it come across me sudden that it was my own self that made Metal Hayes so mad to have me—and all on account of a bit of anger again Dinny. It was at the dance at the crossroads, and I minded well that was the first night me and Dinny spoke serious about marriage. And I was wild in my heart again Dinny, the way he was fixed about the farm, and the old aunt keeping such a tight hold on him.

So when Metal Hayes comes up and asks me, I looks at him encouraging and says, 'Yes,' out of spite again Dinny. Dinny turns away quick, and I'm sorry for a minute. But it turns out well. For Hayes is all excited, thinking himself a great wonder with the women, and he swings me round quick, and dances very fast, the way those mountainy men do get that don't be going out to dances much. And in a little while he's making a proper show of himself, doing capers all by himself. And then I looks to see Dinny, and he's laughing. And I has to laugh too. And sudden I'm over my spite again him. And as soon as we can, we slips away from the dance, and cycles off together, real good friends.

But Metal Hayes is real took with me from that time, though I never had no mind for him, him being older. I had no fancy for his loud-mouthed ways and the small eyes he had, dug real far underneath his brows, with a look in them like there was a light behind, as though he was being drove all the time.

But my da, when he knows how it is with Metal, is keen for me to take him, him being a relation on my

mother's side far back, and her coming from around the
Black Mountain the same as himself. And besides, Metal
had plenty put by, as everyone knew well. And though I
knows how my da feels yet I never took it real serious
till that very day.

And as I'm standing there in the cow-house thinking
back, I sees how they come up to the door and stand
waiting for my da to make them welcome.

Then my da comes out in his slow way and stands at
the door.

'God save all here,' says Phil with his big voice.

My da was in his working clothes, the same as he
come in from stooking the corn, in his old grey shirt
and waistcoat. He took them real cool, like as though
he didn't know what brung them. 'Come in, won't ye,'
he says in his soft voice. 'Sure it's a grand evening,
thank God.'

Then they went in, Metal leading the way, and taking
off their caps very awkward, not saying a word. Very
careful my da shut the half-door as though it was real
private.

And it was then it come to me how my life was going
to change by the time the door opened again.

I walks out into the yard and stands there by myself.
Then I thinks, I must get the sop for the morning. And I
goes across the yard and down the haggart to the rick
and stoops down for a sop of the loose straw about the
foot of the rick, for my da to light the fire in the morning.

It was then I began thinking on Dinny. Often and
often I'd told him my da was keen on a match betwixt
myself and Metal, but Dinny made light of it.

'That little old gom of a fella!' And he'd laugh. 'Never fear, girl, it's not you with your red hair and green eyes that will be wanting for a man!'

'We'll have to get married soon, Dinny,' I says to him one evening, 'or my da will be fixing me up with Metal, sure as sure.'

Then he says, 'Wait a bit, Jula girl'—for that was the way he had of saying my name. 'When me old aunt goes I get the place, and there's no one but you I want.'

My da had no mind to have two daughters on his hands in his old age. Norah was backing up my da too—not that she thought much of Metal, for how could she? But she knew well that with me married she'd have things going her own way. And who knew but that some fella would be willing to take her for the place! For my da was a strong farmer with forty acres in the Golden Vein, and not a bit of it mountainy.

After a while I seen the lamp go on in the parlour, for it was dark inside at this time, the thatch coming down and shading the windows.

I thinks to myself, It's time I went in and put on my good dress and drew the rack through my hair. But for the life of me I couldn't bring myself to go in, and shake Metal by the hand, and listen to Phil joking like it was all fixed. And I stands there by the rick like a fool with the sop of straw in my hand till it's real dark and I hears the door open and the scrape of their boots on the yard.

And very quiet, behind their backs, I slips across the cobbles and goes into the kitchen.

Norah has the big three-legged pot on the crane over the fire, boiling up the pig-food ready for the morning.

'Where were you, girl?' she says sharp.

'For God's sake, Norah,' I says quiet, though my heart is beating like a hammer, 'you know I've no mind for him. You know well I've been courting Dinny for the past three years!'

Norah gives her dry laugh, and takes the handle of the bellows and gives it a turn, though the pot is boiling fast. 'You should be thanking God for your good luck, girl! You and your Dinny! I knows his type—hanging around making a big man of himself with the girls, with his bold eye, and his mop of curls—and all the time having a big laugh at ye! That one has no intention of settling down, I can tell you—least of all while that witch of an aunt is above ground.'

I felt myself get real white. 'He says he'll marry me.' My voice was very shook. And Norah stopped turning the bellows and looked up at me real surprised.

'Glory be to God, you haven't been taking him serious, have you?'

I felt the kitchen get darker, like the blood had left my head. 'I'm mad for him, Norah! Mad for him!' I says. 'There's no one else for me, I tell you.'

'Whisht girl!' Norah says shocked. 'I hear my da outside.'

My da come in, walking very slow like he does when he's thinking on something. He stood inside the kitchen and said in his soft way, 'Ye're all in the dark. Light up the lamp now.'

So I pulls down the lamp from the beam and puts a match to it, and I helps Norah take off the big pot and drain the praties. And I watches as my da goes to his own sugan chair inside the hearth and pulls off his boots, looking at each one very careful and serious afore laying it in the corner.

All the time it's as much as I can do to hold myself from speaking, so I fills the kettle and hangs it on the crane, and sits down quiet by the bellows.

And after a while my da hooks his thumbs in his waistcoat and fixes his eyes on the fire and he says, 'I know now you're thinking I was a bit hasty settling the match, Julia girl. But it's time you was settled down. God knows, I won't be here for ever, and I'd like to see you fixed up afore I goes. The years are passing and you're not getting any younger yourself, Julia.'

'Look what happened to me for letting me chances pass me!' puts in Norah, reaching down the mugs and laying the table.

'Let her be! Let her be!' says my da, raising his hand.

'Yes, you let me be—for I won't take that omadhawn of a man for nobody,' I says loud, for the idea of losing Dinny near put me out of my mind. 'I can see myself up there with Metal—with his mud floor, and not a bit of life for miles. I'd be pulling and dragging till the end of me days in that poor place.'

'Whisht, whisht,' says my da, frowning like he always done when anyone got the smallest way roused up. 'He has a fair share of cattle—and sheep too up on the Black Mountain. And a rare hard man when it comes to driving a bargain! He's sober and decent, like his father afore him.'

'I don't care. I'll never take him. Never, never!' I was raging, for I could see my da was set on it.

Very slowly my da laid down his mug and turned and looked at me. 'Compose yourself, girl! You take after your mother's people, wild and headstrong.' Then my da says very earnest, 'I know well you have a mind for Dinny, but there's no chance for you there. That ould aunt of his will live for a good share of years yet, for they come of a long-lived breed. And as long as she's above ground Dinny will never be able to marry.'

'He told me! He told me he'd marry me,' I says.

But my da says, 'I tell you, I'm walking the land at Joe Hayes's one of these days—so let it be, girl!' And he picks up his mug and turns his stocking feet to the fire, and I knows it's no use talking to him no more.

And we sits quiet there waiting till my da has finished his tea; and just the sound of the cricket very faint from behind a pile of sods in the corner, and the tiny falling-in as the ashes turn red.

I don't mind much of my wedding-day—except that early in the morning the tinkers passed, and I mind my da taking a side of bacon down from the hook above the chimney and cutting them a good piece. And I mind them driving off, herself sitting on the tail of the cart holding the child in her shawl, and I wished I was her.

It was Norah that helped me into the blue costume and put on the hat with the little pink and blue flowers and in my hand she put the mother o' pearl prayer-book that I got on my confirmation. Then she stood me in front of the mirror and said she was real pleased with the way I looked.

And I saw there in the mirror, standing out very bright, for it was dark behind in the corner, a girl with dark foxy hair and green eyes, and the palest face I ever did see.

I got into the trap that took me to the chapel like I was dead, although the air was wonderful cool and fresh, and I could hear the bells tolling ahead in the village. The sky was high and clear, like it is in our place, and the Galtys was standing out very blue.

The next thing I mind is kneeling beside Joe Metal. And I sees that he's in a new blue suit. And I notice, seeing him sideways, how his nose is straight at the top and then turns up sudden along about the middle like he had been hit with a hurley. And his pale foxy eyebrows sticks out so that it's hard to see his eyes, they being so deep-set.

He hardly takes a look at me then. And it's only when we're back at the house and are all sitting about the table in the parlour that I sees him look at me sideways, sly-like, out of the corners of his eyes.

But still and all I can't believe he is my husband. And I looks round them all sitting laughing, and codding as though I might see Dinny somewhere among them, with a crowd around him like he always had, talking away all light and airy. And though he wouldn't be looking at me, it would make no matter so long as I could see him. But Dinny wasn't there, as well I knew.

And after the breakfast is over, and the speeches, the priest lights up his pipe and he says to Norah, 'What about a bit of dancing now, Norah? Tell Phil to strike up the fiddle.'

And Phil the Fluter strikes up with the fiddle, for he was good at the reels, and another fella from the village joins in with the gadget.

We dances in the kitchen, it being bigger and more free. Metal and myself starts off and he swings me round in 'The Walls of Limerick' till I feels dizzy.

Every now and then he'd stop off and draw himself a glass of porter, still holding on to my hand and laughing very shrill, and beating time to the music with his foot and shouting to Phil to play faster.

But at last my da gets up from the fire and goes out with some of the men to harness the pony, and I knows it's time for us to be going. I puts on my hat below in the room and they all comes into the yard to see us off, waving and wishing us luck—though they're hoping we'll be gone soon, so they can get back to the dancing.

I hardly pays any heed to Metal all the way, for though he makes a remark now and then and keeps watching my face, I feels that bad I've no mind for the talk.

The day is half through by the time we gets near his place, and when we comes to the boreen that leads to the place, it's like I knew it would be—the boreen narrow and all grown with elderberry and thorn that's twisted about with sticky willie. And it's real lonesome, and the sky isn't high like it is at home, but seems low-down and darksome—like as the mountains was casting a shadow.

The yard was at the end of the boreen, just as if the boreen had widened itself out, and the cobbles was spotted with dung, and clumps of scutch grass grew up again the walls of the house. The house itself was very low-set, and the outhouses broken-down-looking, with a big old three-legged pot lying on its side, half sunk in the ground near the pig-house.

All the time Metal keeps looking at me out the side of his little eyes. Then he tells me to go into the kitchen while he untackles the pony.

Inside it is very dark. But, after a while, I makes out there's a few bits of kindling in the corner, and I puts them on so that soon the fire blazes up.

Then I takes off me hat and looks around proper—and it puts the heart across me.

It was like our kitchen in the size, but so different you could hardly believe it. The bacon hung from the beams, black and dried, like it was a hundred years cured, and when I looks at the dirt floor I thinks as how I'll never be able to give it a good scrub.

I rooted around till I found the kettle and took it out into the yard.

Himself was still there, and I calls to him, 'I'm putting on the tea. Where will I fetch the water?'

He points over his shoulder and I goes across the yard and past him without a word till I sees the path where it leads down through the glen.

And as I'm going down with the kettle in me hand I thinks how it is the wildest place I ever did see, all covered with briar branches and sallys and wild fern and little hard paths winding down through it like goat-tracks. And at the foot is the torrent that spouts from out the Black Mountain and falls into a deep hole beneath, and then runs away across the foot of the glen. The place has a feel about it like you'd never speak out loud, like the rock would come down and crush you. And I dips the kettle in the pool and holds it till it fills up, and I goes up the path quick and into the house.

When I goes in Metal is sitting in the sugan chair, and I puts the kettle on the crane and blows up the fire a bit, and when the kettle boils I gives him his tea. And after a while he whistles up the dog, and goes down the glen, and makes for the Black Mountain beyond, to count the cattle.

And I washes up the ware and sits by the fire and waits. And soon I hears a sound I never hear afore at home—the sound of cooing from the wood-pigeons. Every now and then they'd give their lonesome little 'Coo, coo'. And when I looks out the window it's all bluey below in the glen, like the colour an apron gets when it's faded. And the kitchen is still. And I wonders when Metal's coming back, and what he's thinking out there in the dusk.

I never gets used to it. For it's always like it was from the first—only as winter draws on, it's something terrible, for it's that cold. And the cattle are wild, and kick and rear, so that it's a heart-scald to milk them, as nearly every one of them has to be langled. And all the time there's the baking and the putting-down of the pots of praties for the pigs with no one to help me lift them from the crane, for Metal was all the time beyond in the fields.

At first I wonders how Metal manages the work, for 'tis only at the harvest he hires a man. And then I sees how he can work from morning to night like one possessed, so that they do say below in the village he'd plough by lamplight if he could.

But after a while I knows what drives him. It's like

as if he was trying to put enough in the bank to make up for the place being the way it was, and the way people called him Metal.

After the dinner one day when Metal has gone off to the ploughing again, I sets to and cleans up the parlour—not that there was much could be done with it, it was that gloomy and ugly with the furniture done in black horsehair, and the stuffed bird in a glass box over the mantel. But I sweeps the floor and takes the rug into the yard. And I'm holding it against the wall of the house, giving it a brush, when Norah cycles into the yard.

'Norah,' I says, 'what brung you?' For as soon as I seen her, I seen she was not her own self.

'Come into the house quick,' she says, pushing the bike into the outhouse and looking round to see there's no one in the yard. 'I seen Joe Metal at the ploughing as I come up the boreen,' she says. 'But he didn't see me, for I stayed behind the tree at the corner till he had the horses turned at the headlands, and then I come on quick.'

'What is it, Norah?' I says as soon as we was in the parlour, my heart beating fast, for I knows it's something terrible. And I thinks maybe my da is took sudden with an illness—but never for a moment did I guess at the truth.

'It's nothing, nothing at all, so keep a cool head,' she says annoyed, seeing the look on my face. 'It's nothing but that Dinny's aunt has died sudden, and I wanted to tell you afore Metal would see it in the paper and bring it out sudden.'

'The aunt left him the place in the end, and he's free

now?' I says, to make sure of it, though I feels certain in my mind.

'Now don't take on, girl,' says Norah sharp, for I'd sat down on the hard old couch for my legs wouldn't hold me up no more. 'I knew you'd take it like that! Like you was broken-hearted!'

' 'Twould be no lie to say I was broken-hearted,' I says.

'Don't you be giving way to that kind of talk and disgracing the family,' says Norah.

And she goes on talking away about the aunt, and as how she signed it to him on the death-bed. But I'm not listening, for I'm thinking how now Dinny's free to marry, and here am I up on the mountain married to Joe Metal—as I knew all along it would be!

'Tis a good thing Metal didn't come for his tea till late that evening, for I was sitting there in the parlour crying like me heart would break, long after Norah was gone.

But in the end I comes to myself a bit, and I goes into the kitchen and dashes water on my face to freshen it. And when Metal comes for his tea, I takes care not to put a match to the lamp, but gives him his tea by the light of the fire.

And afterwards Metal lights the lamp himself, and sits by the fire and takes up the paper. And I stays in the shadows washing the ware and making a show of putting the kitchen to rights.

And after a time Metal starts to read out of the paper and to say, 'A shocking accident in Clonmel.' Or, 'They say as how the rates is going up again,' and the like. And I'm answering him, ' 'Tis shocking,' or, 'Do you tell me,' or the like.

Then all of a sudden he says real quiet, 'And I see in the paper as how the old aunt's after dying.' And he looks at me over the paper, but I says nothing, and he says, 'You wouldn't be eating your heart out that you didn't wait for your fine young fella, would you?'

Still I says nothing, and he yells, 'You think I don't know about yourself and Dinny!'

His lips is tight with the teeth showing a bit at the tips, and his little eyes gleaming red-like, way back in his head, as they done when he was angry.

' 'Twas no secret we was doing a line. Sure the whole countryside knew it,' I says, going to the dresser and putting away the ware.

'You're making like it was no more than a bit of sport,' says he, coming up to me at the dresser. 'But don't tell me you wouldn't have married that clown of a fella if you could.'

'Well, that's all over and done with now, Joe,' I says, making believe I don't care what he's saying, though my heart is beating fast.

'Is it! Is it! All over and done with?' he says real wicked, putting his face near to mine. 'You was eating your heart out there when I brung it out. I had me eye on you, and you was eating your heart out.'

'Aren't you my husband now, Joe?' I says quiet.

'I wonder you've the face to stand there and say it,' he says loud. 'And your mind going back to Dinny—and you a married woman.'

'You're not to be saying things like that,' I says sharp.

But Metal shouts, 'And who are you to be laying down

the law about what I'll say in me own house?'

But I don't answer, for once Metal started there was no stopping him. For if he got it into his head you was trying to stop him, he'd go at it the more.

But all the time he's abusing Dinny he does nothing but bring him up afore my eyes as if I could see him plain, with his blue eyes laughing and the lovely way he had of handling the hurley; smooth-like, so that it was like dancing it was that lovely to watch him.

And I turns and looks at Metal where he's leaning against the dresser and he's saying low and wicked, 'You'd like to be out with him ditching this very night, wouldn't you!' And he goes on about how I should be ashamed to be thinking back on Dinny and pining for him.

And I thinks in my own mind, Yes, indeed I do pine for Dinny. And I longs in my heart to be married to him, and not to you!

And it was himself made me that way, for always afore I had been trying to put Dinny out of my mind.

I'm looking intent at Metal while I'm thinking these things, and I sees how his mouth lifts up a bit at the corner in a smile, and I knows he's sure as how I'm taking note of what he's saying. And I thinks to myself, Joe Metal Hayes, you're my husband, and I hates you with my whole heart and soul. And a rage rises up inside of me again him. And it was never quenched, but kept burning slow-like inside of me from that hour.

It was one morning when I went to the turf-shed after Metal had gone to the creamery with the milk-churns that I seen Dinny again.

When I comes out of the shed, I stops a bit and leans again the door, and I feels the cool damp feel of the turf in my arms and the strange dark smell that it has.

And I looks across the glen and the sun is shining gold behind the Black Mountain and setting all the little dewy cobwebs glittering in the hedges. And it's then I hears Dinny's voice saying, 'Jula,' very soft, like he used to.

I looks about every which ways, and I'm that shook that a couple of sods falls from my arms on the ground. Then I sees him, and he's watching me from behind the outhouse, and his eyes laughing.

I steps round the outhouse quick. 'Dinny,' I says, 'what brung you here?'

But he takes the sods out of my arms and he catches me by the hand, and he never stops till we're through the haggart and into the barn.

And inside I can see how he's laughing to himself even though it's dark inside in the barn. For it's the way Dinny always used to have, so that it was as though every bit of him was rejoicing.

Then I says, 'Dinny, for why did you come?'

The smile goes out of his face. 'You know well I come to get a sight of you again.' And then he says, and it was like his old way, 'How is it you never come below for a visit?'

'I've been that busy,' I says, 'I've scarce had time to draw my breath.'

And then I says no more and we stands there a while looking at one another without a word. And 'twas strange, for one time we was so thick there was nothing we didn't say betwixt ourselves. And the way it was with me, I'd have given the whole world if things could have been like they was afore. And I sinks down on the straw for it's like as if I was wore out.

He picks up an old pike that's lying again the post and rubs the mist of dew from the prongs and digs at the ground with it absent-like, and he says, 'Every time I thinks on Metal I wonders how you could have took him. You're not like yourself at all, Jula. The devil's gone out of your eyes.' And he bends down and looks into my face. And sudden he sits down aside me and puts his arms around me. 'If I had my time again, Jula, I'd tell the ould aunt to go to hell. I was surely mad to let you take him.'

And when I sees him close I sees how he's the same as ever he was, and his eyes bright, though I feels old and wore out.

And after a bit, he says, 'Oh Jula, Jula, why did you do it?' And I feels his fingers playing with my hair, and he says it so sad that I feels the tears begin in my eyes. And it's like I'm knowing it for the first time, and I feels the tears pour down my face as he holds me to him.

'Dinny, you don't know what I'd give to be back the way I was,' I says.

'Sure, 'twas all over for us the minute you took him,' Dinny says. 'And now the aunt's dead, there's no one stands betwixt us but himself—and 'twas yourself that made it so.'

For a time we don't say nothing, and I knows I'll remember the smell of the straw and the bitterness I feels in my heart all my life.

'Dinny,' I says, 'isn't it a terror there's no going back!'

And he gives a sigh and he says soft, 'There's no going back for us, girleen.'

But in my heart I'm raging again the way I'm fixed. And it was like the love I had for Dinny had been smouldering like a turf fire whose sparks shower up at the first breath of the bellows. I hates Metal and I longs to be free. And the idea comes to me very clear—there's only Metal now that stands betwixt us. Suppose Metal was to die?

And I says to him soft, 'Tell me, Dinny, if I was free of himself would you take me?'

And he's leaning back in the straw with a sop betwixt his lips, and he says easy, 'For sure, girl, for sure,' absent-like, and I hears the smile in his voice.

Then sudden I hears the straw cracking and he raises himself on his elbow and looks into my face. 'Jula, you wouldn't be thinking—'

But I laughs, making out I'm easy in myself, for not for a minute would I whisper to Dinny what was in my mind. 'For God's sake, Dinny, have some sense,' I says.

He leans back slow, like he's troubled in his mind.

'It's me red head that makes me talk wild the way I do,' I says, trying to sound airy.

And after a while he grows easy and begins codding me like old times. And I make sure to answer him like as near 'twas old times as I can, but all the while the thought do be coming to my mind, like the moth about the chimney of a lamp—suppose Metal was to die! There was only himself betwixt us now! Dinny himself had said it!

For now I wanted Dinny no matter what. For 'twas

like I could read him, and I seen how it was he come to me. 'Twas like a grown man comes back from Ameriky, smiling to himself when he looks on the cabin he was reared in, and thinking on the happy years. But not lonesome in himself for he do be but passing.

But with me it was different—like I had come back sorrowful, tearing the weeds from the mortar, and beating my head on the steps and crying for the door to open again. Like as though I'd have no peace on this earth till I was back in the days that were.

'Twas strange how I felt from that time on.

In the mornings when I'd be following Metal along, pulling the beet for the factory, the wind from the Black Mountain cutting like a whip, and the pair of us dragging at the frozen earth, I'd see him ahead of me creeping along like a little old leprechaun. And I'd feel all still as I planned. 'Twas a terrible hard winter, and the boreen was all rutted where the carts had passed, and the ruts was full of watery clay like skimmed milk. But I paid no heed, for every time I went to the potato-pit or milked the cows or went to the torrent for water my mind was on it, and the feeling of joy I'd get when I thought on him dead. And in the evenings I'd be thinking, soon there'll be no one sitting on that sugan chair, and I'll chop it into kindling and burn it in the fire. And in my heart I'd feel glad, like you do when you'd be looking forward to Christmas.

Then one terrible wet evening with the rain coming down so you could hardly see past the window, I watches him, and I'm careful not to give a sign I have anything in my mind. He takes his time over his tea.

And then he puts a bit of sack over his head, and starts down the glen to have a look at the torrent, for of late he has a great notion that he'll get the electricity put in and be the envy of every farmer hereabouts; for won't he get it free from the torrent and not have to pay a penny piece!

I watches him from the door, my heart thumping again my side, but he don't turn his head, and soon the rain covers him entirely.

I'm careful I don't take my old coat from behind the door, for I knows it will get sopping wet and it would be the first thing he'd see when he come in. So I gets an old bagging apron and puts it about me and slips across to the turf-house.

'Twas dark inside, for the light was near gone. But I knows where the tin of crow poison is and I reaches up where the beam slopes and feels about with my fingers. But I don't find the tin immediate—only the feel of the sticky webs that the spiders has made, all covered with dust, and the skelfy feeling of the rough beam. I shudders with the cold and the fright for the rain is that loud on the roof, and the dripping on the turf pile is slow and lonesome.

Then sudden I feels it, and puts my fingers about it careful, they're shaking that much.

I takes it behind the door where the light comes in a bit through the hinges. And when I have it in my hands, I sees as how it's different from the way I thought on it. For the paper about it is all soft and yellow with the damp, and peeling and hanging from the sides, and the writing isn't bright no more, but blurry and faint and strange, like it was foreign writing, though I knew it wasn't.

The lid is rusted and stuck on tight, but I looks about on the floor and I sees an old nail, and I pushes it under the lid. And at first it won't budge, but I tries again, and sudden the lid springs off and rolls about the floor and into a corner. And when I looks in the tin I sees how the powder is a darkish green colour and all stuck together, so that I thinks, I'll have to scrape it to get enough to kill him.

And then I says to myself, how much will it take to kill a man like Metal? And I thinks on myself scraping the greeny stuff out, and I feels sick with the fright, and I feels my hands sticking cold with sweat to the sides of the tin. And I knows that now it's come to the bit I won't be able to do it. For if I was to give him a big share, he'd taste it for sure. And if I was to give him just a little, wouldn't he be a long time dying! And I was in dread that he'd be lying there on the bed looking at me, and I'd see in his eyes that he knew it was me that done it.

And I knows then that it won't be this way I'll do it.

And it's then I hears the step above the rain, and it's as if the Devil himself appeared afore me, I'm that horror-struck, for Metal's standing there in the door with the sack about his head like a monk.

He says nothing, standing there with the rain spilling down on the sack from the broken gutter, but I sees his teeth gleam wet, and I feels as if I'm going to drop with fright, for it is the most terrible thing I ever seen.

Then he comes up to me and takes the tin from my

hands and when he's near to me I sees how his eyes is jumping and dancing in his head like a demon out of hell.

Sudden he turns about and rushes out to the yard and swings the tin wide like he was sowing wheat and the green stuff spills about in lumps and when the rain drives down on it, it turns bright green and winds about through the cobbles like a snake until it mixes with the brown water from the cow-shed.

And then Metal is shouting and screaming above the rain, but I don't know what he is saying for the roar of the water again the roof is like a torrent.

But as I sees the rain strike down on him, trickling down from the sack over his face, sudden I feels afeared no more, but a stillness comes upon me, for it has come to me how he'll die.

After that it was like he was glad, for he had something again me that he'd never let drop. He'd have a smile on his lips like he was bubbling up with joy that there was no way out for me. And he'd never talk of anything else but that I had a mind to do away with him, so that I dreaded the sight of him coming in.

'You wouldn't be thinking of taking the tongs to me now?' he'd say. 'Or maybe the ould knife there!' And he'd hold out the carver to me, laughing soft to himself. 'There now,' he'd say, 'make a stab at me, do! What has got into you?' he'd say when I'd back away. 'And you such a big woman with the crow poison. Maybe, though, you'd better wait till I do be asleep, and you could creep up and smother me with the ould feather tick.'

And gradual the rage would grow in him, though he'd

be laughing away all the time. And he'd shake and scream at me with his words mixed like he was drunk, 'Kill me, kill me, kill me,' he'd shout out. 'Don't let an ugly ould fella like myself stand in your way.'

I knows then I'll have to do it quick, for he's watching me all the time, and the longer I waits the more he's studying ways of reading my mind. Even when he'd be in the fields I'd see him turn away every now and then and stand still while he'd watch the house and yard for every move I'd be making.

But it never come into his head what I had in mind.

And one evening I gave him his tea very particular and waited till he had drained his mug to the last drop and stretched himself. And without a word, he rose up and went off down the glen. I watched him from the window, and I seen him going down the track, his short butty legs very sure, till the drifting mists that was rising up hid him entirely.

Then I puts on my coat slow, for my mind is made up and nothing would have stopped me. I pulls the lamp down on the rope and quenches it.

The crab-apple tree is twisted and black again the mist like it had been drawn rough on a bit of grey paper with a piece of charred kindling as I takes the track down. I feels my feet slipping on the muck and the fern is sopping with the wet and the briar branches that do crawl wild across the glen tears my bare shins. Here and there I come across a rotting nut from the wild hazels—and everything is all dead and the colour of an old harrow that is left aside to rust.

All the time the little bits of mist keeps hovering and

passing about restless, like they was lost souls looking for a resting-place. And as I creeps down slow the fear of the place gets a hold of me so that when two langled goats spring from behind the grove of sallys I almost lets a scream out of me. But they bounds away and in a minute I can hear them shaking their chains faint and lonesome. 'Tis then I hears the water roaring over the boulders and I knows that I'll come on Metal real soon. And right enough all of a sudden I sees him standing with his back to me on the verge of the hole.

I crouches down behind a boulder, and I waits a bit, but he doesn't turn round, and the feel of the boulder all wet and slippery with the moss, and the sound of the water running cold over the stones, gives me a strange feeling. And sudden I wants to go back up to the house and light the lamp and rake up the fire.

But then I thought on Dinny, and the longing for him rose up in me again. And I gets up sudden and runs up to Metal with my hands afore me. And as I reaches him, he turns and I sees his mouth open and the space between his teeth, and I hears a noise like a screech, but the sound of the water is in my ears, roaring like a train passing. And he staggers and staggers and then his foot slips on the green slime and he falls, flinging up his hands wild, and the water from the torrent beats down on him and I sees where his foxy hair grows dark as the water goes over him.

And I turns and runs back up the glen for I do dread to see his face come to the top and look at me. I feel as if the breath is leaving me, and without knowing it I'm tearing and pulling at the thorn where it catches about my feet, so that afterwards I sees my hands are torn and covered with blood.

When I gets back to the house, I waits by the fire, not lighting the lamp. And all night long I sits there, never stirring but to put fresh sods on the fire, for I was in mortal terror it would go out. But I put no light to the lamp, for the thought come to me that he'd come all drowned as he was, with his face pale like a ghost and his foxy hair all dark and soaking from the water.

But at last the birds begun to sing and, after, the light to come in the sky, and in my heart I knows for sure he's dead and done for, and I feels happy and free, like I was floating on a cloud. And I feels that never no more will I feel bad about anything.

They buries Metal's body in the graveyard behind the church. It's poor land on the verge of the mountain, and the wind cuts down over the bog like it is a knife.

The headstones was all brown and mossy. They was twisted sideways with the scutch grass, pale with hoarfrost, growing wild about them. It had taken a pick to make the grave, the ground was that frozen, and the lumps of clay piled by the grave was frozen together white, like as if a snail had crawled about them. And they made a powerful thudding as the men shovelled them down on the coffin.

And I wonders to myself how long would it be till the grass is high above his grave, like as though he had never been. And I watches the priest standing with the wind tearing at his vestments reading the prayers over the grave. And his finger is laid across the book to keep the pages down, but the thin paper gathers up and beats about his long bony finger back and forth, back and forth, and the prayers are swept away from his mouth and are faint and lonesome one minute and the next loud and sudden so that the words put the heart across you.

The days pass real slow, but I'm content, saying to myself, Dinny'll bide his time now, for it would look a strange thing if he was to come soon after the funeral. And when I sits by the fire at night I thinks of him there below in the valley, thinking of me too and waiting and waiting for the time.

And always when I goes to the shed for a sod of turf, I looks up the boreen wondering when I'll see his dark poll coming around the bend.

And when I sees the wild fern below in the glen pushing through the ground, curled up tight like a baby's fist, and the buds are scattered over the sallys like a mist, something inside me says, Now he'll come. For it's like the whole world was young and airy like Dinny was, and the coldness that was coming into my blood with the waiting goes, for I knows for sure he'll be with me soon.

And one evening when the blossom from the crab-tree is falling slow-like on the ground, I sees him coming up the boreen.

For a while I can scarce believe it's him, for I had thought on seeing him come like that so long. And I stands at the window looking at him and I hears every little sound in the kitchen very clear, and every single thing looks clear and bright to my eyes, like it is cut out of fancy paper.

I draws the rack through my hair to make it tidy, and I goes to the door and waits for him to come into the yard.

And he comes up to me and looks at me steady and I sees how his eyes are like a stone that does be beneath the stream, bluey-grey and dappled when the water moves above it. There's not a bit of change in him and he stands there afore me and we looks at each other without as much as a word.

'And how's Jula?' he says after a bit, and I feels young in my heart again, like I was just beginning, for it was the way he used to say it.

'You've come,' I says, and a sob comes up in my throat.

I sees how the smile leaves his lips and I turns my head away quick, for the tears has sprung to my eyes and I knew Dinny's ways and as how he would turn all cold and suspicious-like if you was too earnest, like as though you was trying to take the laugh out of life, and he wouldn't have it at any price.

And when I looks at him again I sees how he studies my face close, like he was seeing something strange in it.

And I says quick, 'I don't know what come over me—but I'm real glad to see you, Dinny.'

And I sees him smile again, like the danger is past, and I feels my heart soar like a lark, and it's like I'd never tire of the sight of him there with the green buds breaking on the hedge behind and the sky with a tint of blue in it.

Then I recollects myself, and I says, 'Come on in this minute, Dinny, and I'll make you a sup of tea, and you after your journey.' And I gives him a kind of shove, half-laughing to myself, for I thinks, won't it be grand making the tea for Dinny and myself!

'Sit down, can't you,' I says, and I goes about drawing the tea and cutting the soda-cake. And I begins to talk about the parish and how I hear tell as how one was married, and one of the old ones was buried, and the like. And all the time my thoughts is flying ahead about Dinny and myself and the way we'd be together for good.

And as I'm thinking, a terrible fit of lonesomeness grips me sudden, like I was a king sitting up in his palace alone with none of his own kind to talk to. And I thinks to myself, There's not another in the countryside like you after what you done. You're not the same girl, nor ever will be again. But I hands Dinny the mug of tea and I thinks to myself, Maybe after the years pass by and Dinny and me are on the farm together, it will all fade like as it had never been.

I takes a mug myself and sits across from him. And I says soft, 'Many's the time I thought on us like this, Dinny, but it was like you'd think of heaven, real far off. But now it has come to be.'

But he don't look at me, but sits there with the mug in his hand, awkward-like, and his face turned to the fire.

'Is it the way you're worried about coming up here and people talking?' I says. 'There's no call to be thinking and pausing over that, for they all knew well it was me you was always great on, and now Metal's gone there's no hold on me.'

But he made no answer, but took up the spoon and begun stirring his tea slow.

And though I knows well how he hates being tied down, still I has to know for sure, and I says, 'When the

harvest comes there'll only be us two, and I'll bring the
tea out to the fields, and we'll laugh and talk like we
used to. And when winter draws in, we'll be across the
fire from each other, peaceful and content, and it'll be
like it should have been from the start—'

I looks up and my heart turns like it was froze, for there
is something in his eyes that I never seen afore.

'Dinny!' I says. 'Dinny—' I says again.

But he spoke up like he was talking to a stranger. 'I
heard about your trouble, Jula, and I come to say I feels
for you—they all do below at home.'

And the way he says it I knows well what he is thinking. 'Do they feel for me below?' I says dry. 'Or is it the
way they think as how I pushed him in?'

I hears him draw in his breath sharp at the rough way
I brung it out, and he says quick, 'Oh, sure, there's
always a few bad-minded ones.' He looks down at the
mug in his hand and it trembles a bit and some tea slops
over on his wrist.

I says, straight and plain, 'Do you think I done away
with him? Speak your mind.'

Then he looks at me and he shudders and he sets the
mug down on the floor slow, and I knows he's thinking
on me creeping up on Metal and pushing him into the
torrent, and he feels like he can hear Metal's screeching
in his ears as he falls.

And sudden I knows 'twas all for nothing I murdered
Metal. For even if I was to swear to Dinny afore God on
my bended knees that I didn't, yet he would be feared
to believe me.

'And what do you think yourself, Dinny? Do you

think I done it?' I says quiet, though I feels my lips dry
as I speaks.

'God, no, Jula girl! Sure I knows you better than that,'
he says quick, but his voice is hoarse and I sees how his
eyes is frightened.

And I says, 'You'd never marry me now, not in a
thousand years.'

'I would!' he says earnest. 'You're the only girl I
ever loved.'

Then I says, 'You don't know what love is, Dinny.
You don't know what it is to sit by the chimney with
Metal across from you, thinking and thinking, When the
smoke goes up it'll blow across the valley over my own
place, but I'll never be free, never till the day the man
across the fire from me is dead.'

He jumps to his feet sudden. 'Jula, Jula, say you
didn't do it!' he calls, and he looks real afeared. And the
face I thought so handsome looks soft and weak to me
now, for I had done murder and felt different.

'You're craving the answer because you're thinking
to yourself, Julia killed her man for me, because she
thought I'd marry her, and when I come to draw my last
breath, will I be held responsible for the murder that
was done? That's what you're afeared of in your heart.
And it's right you should!' And my voice is loud and I
hears it speaking apart from myself. ' 'Tis only right
and proper you should, for I done it for you. I did! I
did! I did!'

He backs away from me again the chair so that the
mug spills on the floor and the tea hisses again the
fire. And he takes a grip of the chair and he's shaking and

twitching like one with the ague.

Then he goes slow across the kitchen. And I watches him as he goes through the door, the evening light touching him a minute and lighting up his face.

And as he's crossing the yard, sudden it come to me that he's going out of my life for good and all. And a terrible rage grips me now that I knows I done it all for nothing. And I sees behind the door the shotgun Metal kept again the foxes getting at the poultry, and I feels a sort of wild joy as I takes it up. And as Dinny passes the bit of the ditch that is broken I rises the gun to my shoulder like I seen Metal do. I never touches that gun afore and it jerks and bobs about in my hands as I fires.

When the terrible noise is past Dinny don't move nor speak, but I sees him turn his head slow and look at me, like as if he saw something behind me. Then I sees the blood trickle down from his dark poll and spill across his hand as he makes to catch at the ditch, and I sees him fall to the cobbles.

I goes slow towards him, for it's like I go to my own death now that he is gone. His face is hid but I sees his hand flung out and half-curved in a pool of water that spills betwixt his fingers like milk.

The yard is lonesome and empty and I sees a tuft of straw sticking on the prongs of a pike again the outhouse and moving a bit in the breeze.

The hedges is shadowy and now the light is going from the sky, and the gold and red is coming up in the distance with all the colours mixed faint, like in the inside of one of them roses you see climbing about a ditch, and the smells that comes up off the land makes me mind all the things in my life, every small thing. And sudden I sees myself going to school in the morning with my satchel and the whitethorn in bloom, and the dew bending the blades of grass on the verge of the road, and the air all cool and sweet with the scent of things that grows in the ditches.

And I feels an awful grief come up in me slow for all them things that is past and gone and will come no more. For it's like this I'll be for ever more, remembering things about myself in little lonesome pictures—like you do about them that are on the altar-list of the dead.

The Rescue Brigade

FRED SCOTT

An oral reminiscence collected, transcribed and edited by Nigel Gray.

AFTER I got my deputy's ticket they would have us join the rescue brigade. 'We want a good man on the rescue brigade.' That was the cry. So I went with the rescue brigade. I had a lot of work doing with them. Then in 1940 I had a duodenal ulcer burst. I came to bank one day and I had such an awful pain you'd think there was a knife right through us. The trams was running on the main road then. And I decided to call in at the doctor's when I got off the tram. It was half past five at night and I went into the doctor's. I didn't get into surgery. He came into the waiting-room. He said, 'What's the matter with you?' I told him about the pain.

Anyway it's about half past eleven at night and I'm in the pit when this feeling come on us again. And I didn't know whether I wanted to vomit or what I wanted to do. I had a terrible feeling. And the gaffer says, 'We'll run you in on the set. But where am I going to get anybody to replace you now at this time of night?'

I says, 'Well, you'll just have to fiddle on, Tommy, till you get somebody. I'm ill, man.'

He says, 'I'll away to bank, man, and I'll get a pot of

tea for you.' So he's away to bank and he come back with a pot of tea with a drop of rum in it. But I never see the coal-face that day.

I comes out and when I come out it was pay-day. I says, 'I'll away up and get my pay.' And I away up and I gets my pay. 'By,' I says, 'I feel champion. That pain's went off.'

I went to work again that night for Saturday morning and the under-manager says, 'How are you feeling the day?'

I says, 'I've got a lease of new life. I feel champion now.'

But the Saturday night I was getting ready to go to the pictures and this feeling came on us again. And then whoosh! Blood! What a mess. Send for the doctor. Ambulance and away. So I gets into hospital. And the doctor says, 'Well, I'm sorry, you're too far gone. You've been neglected. We can't do a thing with you bar take you in and give you a bed.' So that's what they done. So the next morning when he came down the ward he says, 'You still here yet?'

I says, 'Aye, I'm still here.' And he's shaking his head. And the next thing I knew they're putting a screen around the bed and here's the vicar praying with us. And I broke down a-crying then.

And I just seemed to float to the ceiling. And I was looking back at mysel' lying in the bed and there was the man kneeling there praying at the bedside. And I just seemed as if I turned and away down the corridor and I couldn't see like for the tears and that that were streaming from me face. It was a long way down the corridor

when I hears them shouting, 'Fred Scott! Fred Scott!'
And I looks back and I see the lights following me from
the cap lamps. But they were a long way off and I kept
on my journey. And as I got on the road I sees in the
distance the light from a door or open window. And as I
advanced towards the light there was a woman's hand
and a voice and she says, 'I'll help.' And that was it. I
was out of that corridor into another corridor. It was a
bit brighter but as I went into the garden I started
arguing and fighting with somebody. Who I was fighting
with I don't know but I laid the law down right, left
and centre as I went down this garden. And then I came
to the most beautiful garden that I'd ever seen. There
was banks and banks of flowers both sides. And there
was the straight and narrow path. And I walked a long
way down. I says, By, what a long way down here. I've
never seen a garden this length without cross paths or
something. But no. I kept marching on and marching on
and then there was a bend in the path. As I got around
the bend I says, We're coming to somewhere here now.
There was a group of people sitting and they were sitting
at some gates and as I approached them they got up and
looked back at me as much as to say, 'By, you haven't
half been some time in coming. Wherever have you
been?' And it just seemed as if they pulled their shrouds
up, and away towards these gates. And I says, Oh, we're
coming somewhere now. The group of people troops
around the half-gate and as I got towards the gate the
gate comes and it closes against us. I says, What funny
people closing the gate against us, and seeing us coming.
They are funny blighters. Where am I? And I'm looking

up above to see there's any name or owt above the gate. And I couldn't see as if like for the sun. And I'm trying to shield my eyes and here's Christ's face appears through a great wreath of laurel leaves. And there was the golden ringlets hanging like down to his shoulders and you could see rough hair and rough beard but you could see the skin of a young man burnt red, red with the sun, and the big hooky nose on him, and the lovely clear blue eyes, and you'd think he was penetrating the inner thoughts. And that was it.

When I come to on the bed there was a nurse sitting there and she's rubbing my hands and she says, 'By, you haven't half been away some time. Wherever have you been?'

I says, 'Hinny, you'll never believe us.' And I was a long time before I ever dared tell anybody.

In 1947 I was with the rescue brigade and I was at Whitehaven disaster. I was called for to go and I went away from here like twelve o'clock in the day and I was picked up by the fire tender and taken away down to the pit. When we got there it was like dinner-time. 'Oh, you canny get into the pit yet. There's so many in and there's so many out.'

I says, 'Right, give me a couple of blankets. I'll be laying over there in the sand. Just give us a call when you want us because I've been to work. Foreshift.' And I just went and I lay on the sand.

Of course the Salvation Army were there and they were dishing out pies and pop and different things. And I says to my mates, 'You want nowt to do with nowt. Dinna eat owt at all. Because you don't know what we're going to come up against when you get down there.'

'Aw, we'll be all right. These are for nowt.'

I says, 'Right, you carry on, but Freddy wants nowt.' I didn't have a bite.

At twelve o'clock at night they come. 'Away, lad. It's time you were down the pit.' They shook me. Got me up. That was it. Down we goes. The rescue team. Stretcher-bearers. Water-carriers. Different ones carrying the gear because every team has like a full pack for to carry. You've got your own apparatus to attend to. You've got a bottle of liquid oxygen. Tripods and canisters, and things for filling the apparatus up when you get to the far end. It's filled with caustic soda. Now when you're breathing your breath goes through that caustic soda. It mixes with the cold air that you put into the liquid oxygen. It would burn you if it wasn't mixed with your own breath.

We get down the pit. They had a set for to put the gear in. We gets the set loaded and I gets into the tub and all. I says, 'Right, in we get.' And away it went. A lovely ride for so far till it must have come to like the sea bed and then it went down and as soon as it went over the top they were jumping out. They got the wind up, some of them. I said, 'It's all right. It's went this way before. It's not just changing now.' So I got a ride as far as possible. What had happened with the explosion was the ropes had been cut at that point. I gets out of the tub and takes the apparatus out and walks on by myself. They other lads had to follow on after the set. I said, 'Are youse ready?'

'Aye, aye, everybody's ready.'

I was advancing and here's this fall of stone. It was undescribable the height of the fall of stone. But I climbs up on to the top. It's only about a yard high like on the top. And with that little spotlight I was carrying you could see for far enough. And of course I just kept advancing, never dreaming about the others, thinking they were following, you see, till I hears this 'Fred Scott! Fred Scott!' And my mind flowed back, right back to 1940. My mind flew back to that day in infirmary and this was it exact. I looked back and there was the lights. And there I was standing by myself like and at that moment if they'd have put the needle in us I don't think they'd 've got blood out. I was froze with the shock.

Then I continues on my journey and I was off the top of the fall and down and there were just two or three yards and then over on the top of another fall and down again. It was a terrible journey in, like, with falls all over the place. The destruction, it was undescribable. We come to this fresh-air base. We got our puffs there at the fresh-air base and of course I looks up and looks at the lamp. I says, 'By, fresh-air base! We shouldn't be in here.' There was 2½% and the lamp was hanging four or five foot off the top. I says, 'By! there's some juice in here all right. What have we let ourselves in for now?' I hears this hushing, hushing, farther up. I says, 'Is that a borehole?'

He says, 'Nay, there's no borehole here.'

I says, 'What's that noise?'

He says, 'That's the blower.'

I thought it was a hole drilled from another seam and

it was the water coming from another seam, this whiissshhh, by the sound of it. But it was the gas blower. 'Well,' I said, 'we have let ourselves in for something here.' So we comes back to the fresh-air base and we takes our boots off and puts rubber boots on. Put rubber gloves on. And get air apparatuses filled up. Then Joe Soap, me, shoved on along in front.

The captain said, 'There's four bodies along there. Go in and see what you can do but keep two paces apart. Don't catch the sides.' Don't do this. Don't do that. 'There's hoardings up in front of you. Careful when you're getting through the hoardings.' That was for the air to blow the gas away off. 'You're in a dangerous atmosphere.'

So I says, 'Right.' So we gets through this canvas door. I advances in and I gets right up to the face engine and here here's the face engine and here's the first body lying. He was naked as the day he was born. The only things that was left was the short sleeves that was fastened on. His belt on. Everything else was off him. The surprising part about it was the detonators and powder that was left lying. You would have thought that would have went off. And it never did. He was a deputy because there was hundreds and hundreds of caps lying and they were just as if they were straight out the shop. Clean as a whistle. Not a mark on them.

I just takes and gets the shroud. A canvas shroud that I had. Puts the shroud down and pulls him over on to it. The next thing I knew everybody's away. Flew. I says, What's happened with that lot? Anyway I just takes and putters on and wraps him up in the shroud and put the number off his lamp, like, 57, and marks it on the canvas shroud on the top. And rolls him on to the stretcher and straps him so that he wouldn't come off.

Then one man came back to me and motioned—he couldn't speak, you see, without the apparatus being on—but motioned that he'd vomited at the site. This was all the free stuff that they was getting into them. I warned them what would happen but they were all getting it for nowt. They takes and whips that one up and I just gets myself underneath and I looks and there was another one lying there so I throws the shroud in first and gets mysel' in. This feller was like lying and his hands was towards the belt where the belt lifted up so the coals would lift into the truck that was standing in the main gate. He was lying like that and of course when I pulled him back to pull him on to the shroud I thought, Has he got gloves on? because his fingers came away with the weight of the belt, you see. And there was just the bone left. And with me doing that, the feller next to me, he vomited. And he was away out. And that just left us two men. And they wanted to be away. And I looks at my gaffer and I says, 'You want to be away an' all. Gerron. I'm here to do a job. If you want to gang, gang. That's it.' But they said like if I was stopping they would stop with us. So we got over the top of the conveyor to the face and here's another two lying at the face. But oh they were in a terrible state, like, these two. You could taste it even though you had the apparatus on. Anyway we gets them dressed up and that and their numbers on to the sheet. They were bursted with the force of the explosion. I had to burn all me clothes when I got finished with that job.

Then I had a look to see if there was owt else lying about. I just gets in under the other side of the face. And there was another one hanging. On the other side of this face it had been shaker pans that they had, you see. The pans were about ten foot long. And they'd had a pan off and they'd had it on top of the other pan. This had happened on a stone-stripping shift. There was a fall of stone right where this man was and when the explosion went off the pan had lifted him and he must have been standing like straddle-legged over the top of the thing when it had went off because he was partly buried with the fall of the stone and with the next pan being in the cradle the pans had just shot up with the weight of the stone and lifted him and he was fast by the feet and hung up.

Well, we put bars and things to try and ease it off, like, but we couldn't do nowt with him like. So I says, 'Have you got a knife?' Naebody had a knife. So I said, 'Gan on and seek a knife.' And I sent him away back to the fresh-air base and he come back with a penknife. So I just took and I cut him out. That was all I could do, like to get him out, you see. I takes and cuts him off the conveyor. I cut the boots and everything and stripped them down off. But they would have nowt to dae with us. They left me. Till I shouted to them, like, that I had him out, you see. And that was it. And of course away he comes. But I didn't venture any further than that. I says, 'Well, the inquisitiveness is gone from us now. That's it. I'm off.'

We gets out and away to another pit for to get washed

and such-like and get a feed. And the next I knew we were in the workhouse. I said, 'I've often wondered what it's like in the workhouse.' And by! everybody was dying for a pint. I couldn't explain the feeling that there was for to have a pint.

This morning we gets up and they give us our breakfast. A cup of tea, anyway, and a bun they gave us. Then we went on this bus to the pit canteen for our breakfast. And the bloke who was driving the bus, it was his mother-in-law who was the manageress in the canteen. And you know that funny twang that the Ashington lads have. He says, 'Why, tha knaws, lad, every time tha gans into that canteen it's chips and pies, and pies and chips. I've had that many chips since I went in there that I've got a square arsehole.'

Well, we're coming down the bank from this workhouse and I'm looking out the window and I say, 'Looka there. Looka there.' And there's a hand pulling the pints. Well, my mate and me we jumped off the bus, the two of us, and away. Of course everything was fastened off. We hadn't to be in the pubs or nowt. But we jumped off the bus and were away in there.

Soon as we got in there was a bloke standing at the bar. 'Oh,' he says, 'the Geordies.' Because I just asked for a pint, you see. He says, 'Are you on the rescue brigade?'

I says, 'Oh aye, on the rescue brigade.'

'Well, that one's on me.' And he stood the pint. He was from the south somewhere, like Sussex or somewhere. Of course he was quizzing us lads but he didn't get nowt out us like. We daresn't tell nowt, you see. We keep quiet about these jobs, you see. So I gets the pint. Well, I tell you it never left my lips. That one pint straight off. The bloke was well-nigh flabbergasted. He said, 'Fill them up. I've never seen a pint gan as quick.'

We had three pints apiece. The manager at the back of the bar give a pint. And that was it. So when we gets down to the pit for to start, the inspector's standing there. 'Get away back and get your clothes on. Get out!' Sacked and finished.

By! I'll never forget that do.

I'm just waiting now till I come to the beautiful garden. I've still got that to come.

The Facts of Life

JAMES STERN

I

WITH her delicate, china-like complexion, her gleaming auburn hair, her fame in the hunting field, it would have been remarkable had my mother lacked admirers. As a child at home in Ireland I assumed, quite rightly, that her most loyal male friends were the few men who lived alone, those bachelors who appeared at Bective, sometimes on weekdays for tea, but as a rule on Sundays, for luncheon. I could not help observing that these visitors treated me with a certain consideration, an undemonstrative concern, to which I was unaccustomed. Of these regulars the most memorable figure was that of Uncle Jack—who was not a real uncle, but the brother of Tom Holford, who had married my mother's one sister.

Uncle Jack lived in one room of a pub in Our Town, as we called the market town of Navan. It was only four miles from Bective, and Uncle Jack would turn up at almost any hour, in any weather, and always on a bicycle. To everyone in Navan, in our area of the County Meath, he was The Captain, and even there, in Ireland, considered a 'wee bit quair'.

Memories of this man are even older than the hunting-crop that hangs on the wall beside me as I write; round its shaft on a band of silver, in his hand, is inscribed my Christian name and the date: XMAS 1910. The gift was as characteristic as the inscription that lacks the name of the donor. Of himself Uncle Jack thought little. Of those in whom he detected a sign of pretence, of pomp or snobbery, he thought less; from such folk he withdrew. On the peasant, the sick, the poor, he would pay calls; and on their chimneys, when their backs were turned, leave behind a packet of tea, a twist of shag, half a crown. And on the young, by the warmth of a handshake, a hug, he would lavish an unspoken affection which they instantly recognised, reciprocated, cherished, and never forgot. At Christmas and on birthdays he also gave them presents, the like of which, however small, no one else, least of all the children, had thought of, and which would prove to fulfil a hitherto unconscious dream.

Had he not possessed such qualities, Uncle Jack at first sight might have inspired fear rather than affection. A child might take one look, stare, and contemplate flight. Even at Bective, with its high Georgian doorways, he had to lower his head on the threshold of each room. When you placed your hand in his, it was like having half your arm engulfed in the mobile branches of an oak. The skin, even of the palm, felt like bark. But what surprised and delighted me, as much as they disgusted my parents, were Uncle Jack's clothes. Instead of a suit for the Sabbath, he would appear in cast-off army breeches, frayed puttees, hobnailed boots, a topcoat with a length of rope where a belt once had been. His tweed jackets

had elbows upholstered in brown leather and pockets
specially made to hold 'a brace of rabbits apiece'. Round
his neck above a khaki shirt he generally wore a large
cotton bandana, whose original colours had long ago
faded into a state of beauty. Except in the hunting field,
he never covered his head. In my memory he seems
invariably to have arrived at Bective in a downpour of
rain.

'Oh, Jack, really!' my mother would repeat each time.
'You must be drowned! You'd better go and change!'

For answer he would stand on the stone floor of the
porch, and there, for an instant, allow the water to drip
from his hands and shoulders as from the branches of a
tree. Then, like a dog from a river, he would give his
round, close-cropped head a violent shake. As the rain-
drops sprayed off it over the porch, my mother for
refuge would dart behind the glass door into the hall.
Then from his breast-pocket he pulled another bandana.
Seizing it like a towel in both hands, he would start
furiously rubbing his head, his face. Only when satisfied
that both were dry would he utter a word, or a grunt. But
whichever it might be would sound so unlike a normal
human voice, so deep, so like an echo in a cave that, no
matter how long you had known him, it invariably took
you by surprise. You would glance up, and there see
again what, at first sight, must have given the unwarned
adult a shock. Uncle Jack had no nose. . . .

To his mouth he also had no roof. Where the nose once
had been, there was now a hole. For he did, at one time,
have a nose. Until towards the end of the Boer War.
Before I was born. In that war a Savage—a word denoting

an African Negro, so that for years I assumed that Boers were black—had attacked Uncle Jack with an assegai. With assegais we were familiar, for Uncle Tom had a sheaf of these venomous-looking weapons among the walking-sticks and umbrellas in the hall at Kilcairne. Although Uncle Jack had finally strangled the Savage 'with his own bare hands', there had been a long and desperate struggle in which, owing to the white man's valour, his superior strength, he had not only saved his life, he lived to win the admiration of his regiment and lose nothing but his nose. If you looked 'carefully', you could still see the remains of the scar made by the Savage man's razor-sharp spear.

By children, above all by those who recoil instinctively from violence, such stories are not forgotten: they sink deep into the imagination. To me, needless to say, this warrior became a hero.

Like all proper heroes and most big men, Uncle Jack was very gentle, especially towards animals and the young. If horses can be said to resemble human beings, Uncle Jack's string of hunters did bear a likeness to their owner. The least tall measured from its withers to the ground seldom less than seventeen hands. Uncle Jack did not believe in clipping their coats for the winter, nor in plaiting their manes or tails. What he did believe in was patience. By patience and perseverance he proved that most horses can be persuaded to do anything a four-legged animal is capable of doing at all. On their looks alone no coper would have offered a tenner for any one of them. Even at meets, on frosty winter mornings, they had no sparkle in their eyes; standing on three legs, their unkempt heads would droop like those of drudges kept by tinkers. From this perhaps blissful state of lethargy, neither hunting-horn nor hound could rouse them. Such was their tameness, so soft their mouths, that to steer and stop them a single snaffle on a single rein sufficed. And when dismounted and left to their own devices, even in the middle of a hunt with hounds giving tongue and other horses galloping past, these camel-like creatures would stand still, lower their heads, and begin, regardless, to graze.

I talk as though I know from experience. I do. For in our holidays my brother Reggie and I exercised and hunted these animals. And those with some knowledge of foxhunting will not need to be told what manner of man offers to mount children on his own horses! Had we ridden these lanky, magically trained beasts before being put astride our wild-eyed, excitable, over-fed ponies, what a nerve even I might have developed in the saddle!

One of the few feats Uncle Jack had failed to think of persuading his horses to perform was to sit on their haunches or lower themselves circus-wise on to their knees. We should then have been able to manage without a mounting-block. This problem, however, Uncle Jack soon solved: he equipped the horses we rode with a rope ladder fastened to the saddle. At meets, dressed unbelievably in pink or black coat and topper, this huge man would stand at our side. 'No, the mane, old boy!' he would boom. 'Grab it! That's what it's there for! Now face tailwards. Left foot on the ladder. Right hand on the saddle-flap. That's it. Now one, two—up you go!'

And once he had seen us mounted, he took no more responsibility, except to add: 'Now, for God's sake, don't follow me. Follow that mother of yours. *If you can. . . !'*

If we could! Uncle Jack knew. He knew what it was like to follow our mother. Across country. When scent was good, and hounds screaming. *He* did not try. And for a sound reason. My mother rode horses that, had she allowed them to go into training, might well have stood a chance of winning the Grand National Steeplechase at Aintree. Uncle Jack's animals, even with six instead of sixteen stone on their backs, could not be persuaded to change from a canter into a gallop, for to gallop they had never been asked.

It was said in Ireland by all manner of people that no woman, and few men, had ever ridden across the green fields of Meath as 'straight' as our mother. Of those few men Uncle Jack was surely one. Some who professed not to like him—those in whom he had sensed a sign of vulgarity or pretentiousness and whose ire he may have aroused by turning his back—called Uncle Jack's hunters 'those ill-bred circus nags' and their owner 'the farmer's curse'. For when the fox had broken covert, and the pack had picked up the scent; when the master or huntsman had been seen to raise his cap, and the horn had been heard; when a field of two hundred mounted men and women had begun to charge for the nearest gate or gap and our mother, already in the lead, was reining in Cremore or Otter to face the only 'possible-looking' place in the otherwise unjumpable hedge, a spectator on his feet might see, out by himself, a pink- or black-coated figure on a huge shaggy chestnut loping towards the densest, most impenetrable thicket of thorn. The on-looker might observe that on approaching it the chestnut would break from the lope to a trot, from trot to a walk, and then with its ears back, head down, the horse would slowly bulldoze its way through the fence, to vanish with its rider on the other side. And should there be a wide Meath ditch beyond, the horse would drop leisurely into it, walk along it, then heave itself out at the most suitable spot. And should the spectator follow the hunt a little further, he might notice a second horse, as tall and shaggy as the first, approach the same fence in the same place and there negotiate the obstacle in identical fashion. And instead of a man on that horse, there would be a small, white-faced boy in brown tweed coat and bowler hat.

Riding to hounds in such a manner had, of course, one serious drawback: should the hunt be fast and of brief duration, Uncle Jack could seldom hope to be 'in at the death', or close to hounds when they lost the scent and 'checked'; whereupon the white-faced boy would be even further in the rear—and in trouble. Upon my catching up with the pack at last, my father would demand my reason for not having followed either my mother or himself, while the former would wish to know 'why on earth' I had not followed my father. 'Look at Reggie! He got here long before you!'

It was a familiar refrain. From experience I had learned that to follow any stable-companion of the pony I happened to be riding was to court disaster, was asking to be 'run away with'. A fresh animal—and ours, fed on oats, were always fresh—will invariably attempt to bolt in the wake of a horse from the same stable. Uncle Jack's shaggy beasts, however, could not have bolted if they had tried, and they certainly could not have remained five minutes within sight of my mother; what did make these lamb-like creatures cock an interested ear was to be allowed to lope peacefully along after their master and their friend, the animal he rode. Thus in the tense hush of the crowd at covert-sides, mounted on one of these hunters, I used to find myself repeating with fervour a most surprising prayer: 'Please God, let this hunt be any kind of hunt You wish, but—please—let it be *long!*' For if I did manage to get to the end it mattered little to my parents, in their first flush of family pride, on whose heels their elder son had followed or how he had managed to achieve this unlikely feat. There would be mutual admiration then; smiles all round—the closest my parents ever came to a demonstration of encouragement of anything I attempted to do.

II

To continue this narrative I must now pass on from this man I had learned to love and respect, to a place in which he would have cut a more incongruous figure than anywhere else I can think of. In time I must also pass over some of the grimmest years in Europe's history, for I know that the Armistice had been signed, that my father had returned from France to Bective, and that I had been at Eton something like a year. But the place was not Ireland. It was my grandmother's house in Kensington. She herself was there, in the morning-room, and so was her eldest son, my father—when, without her customary warning, Grandma rose from her chair and left the room. Taken for once by surprise, I began searching desperately for an excuse to escape, to avoid being caught alone in the same room with my father, when my efforts were shattered by the most dreaded of words.

'Look here,' I heard my father say, 'I want to see you in the library.'

Dreaded these words would have been anyway, but by a Lower Boy at Eton they were doubly feared, for this was the phrase that was uttered—'Stern, you are wanted in the Library'—when serious trouble brewed, when some law had been broken, some crime detected, and senior members of the house had decided to take justice out of the hands of adults into their own.

As I followed my father across the marble hall I noticed that in one of *his* hands he held some papers, among them a thin book or pamphlet with a brown paper cover. Although highly suspicious by nature, it evidently had not occurred to him that I might make the reckless attempt, as we moved from one room to the other, to read the title on that cover. Although not wholly successful—the only words I managed to read being ADVICE and SCOUT—the effort did provide a clue. So, as I stepped behind him into the library (a room even gloomier than that which went by this name at school), I began preparing myself for the imminent ordeal.

'Sit down,' my father said.

It soon became clear that this was just what he longed to do, but could not. As I pretended to be sitting comfortably in a corner of the sofa, he lowered himself before me on to the fender-seat, the papers and pamphlet in his outstretched hand, his head down, only an instant later to get up, to walk to the window. And from there, with his back to me, gazing out at the foggy London scene, he began in a series of jerky, half-finished sentences, to mumble:

'You're growing up, y'know . . . not long before you'll . . . you'll be—well, grown up. Hard for me to believe . . . seems only yesterday, but—well, there it is. You'll be in the Army Class soon. Only another year. Then Sandhurst, of course. To pass in there—it means work, y'know. . . .'

He turned. And started pacing up and down behind the sofa on which I sat.

'In my opinion,' he began again, his voice rising a little. 'In my opinion you—don't seem to me—o' course I may be mistaken—but it seems to me you—er—don't take life seriously enough. You did, I know, while I was out in France, pass into Eton. But you passed in pretty low, y'know. Your reports—they aren't exactly—er—something to write home about. "Concentration poor" . . . "seems to spend a lot of time dreaming. . . ."'

'As I was saying, you got to take—er—life seriously. You're the eldest. It is expected of you to—er—well, set an example. Stands to reason. The point is you—you'll soon be a man. Now, o' course I can't lead your life for you. I can only point out the—er—the straight path.

You've had everything a child could wish for. You happen to have been born in Ireland. A pity. However, no good crying, as they say, over spilled milk. In any case, you're an Englishman—and I trust you'll never forget it. Soon after your birth I put you down for the best school in the country. I've done all I can. It's up to you now. The most important thing in life is to keep straight. . . .'

The voice faltered, trailed off, failed. This was by far the longest speech I had ever heard my father make. I was so nervous, as much on his account (I kept thinking he might suddenly break down) as on mine, that sweat had broken out in the palms of my hands. I glanced up. He had returned to the window again; but by the position of his head, his elbows, I could tell that he was no longer gazing out, that instead he was studying the papers or the pamphlet in his hands. All of a sudden he whirled round, took a step toward me, and in a far louder, almost menacing tone, he began to bark: 'You'll run into temptations, y'know. Can't avoid 'em. You'll turn yer back on 'em, o' course. If you're worth yer salt. There are wrong uns in every school, even the best. Have nothing to do with 'em. Got to be careful who ya make friends with. Better have none than wrong uns. Even get into th'Army, wrong uns do—'

He was coming nearer. Because my eyes were lowered I could see the polished brown caps of his shoes on the red and blue pattern of the carpet. Hypnotised, I watched the shoes move towards me.

'Women, too!' the voice suddenly blurted out. 'There are women, y'know, who can give a man—er—can ruin a young man, fer life—'

He stopped abruptly. And in a low shocked voice, as though it had suddenly occurred to him I might have fallen asleep, he asked: 'I say! You listening?'

His nearness compelled me to glance up. He was standing over me.

'Yes,' I said.

Whereupon his body suddenly shot into the position of attention. Arms rigid, he glared, then made that grimace which turned him into a man I felt I did not know. In a steady voice, the steadiness of a man taking careful aim, he said: 'You—you don't want to look like Jack Holford, do ya?'

III

Since that day in my grandmother's London house I learned, at intervals over the years, several things about the man whom I continued, all his life, to love and admire. To me the most interesting fact to emerge was that Uncle Jack had been engaged to marry my mother. Her family, however, had intervened. It had been brought to their ears that there appeared to be something very wrong with their daughter's fiancé. And one day in the hunting field he had indeed been found in a ditch, suffering from violent convulsions. Among the men who helped to pull Jack Holford out of the ditch that day, to escort him to hospital, and to hear his affliction diagnosed as epilepsy, had been my mother's eldest brother, Uncle Sam.

Uncle Jack lived nevertheless to be eighty years and

more, a never-complaining martyr to arthritis, to a body bent and racked by perpetual pain. Of his last years several were spent—and more dangerously than in the hunting field—in a self-propelled wheelchair on the roads and lanes of Dorset. As well as painful, his daily outings— in rain, snow, and gale—would also be slow, for few pedestrians, cyclists, or children, seeing him on the road, would fail to stop and talk to the hunched, hatless, undauntable bundle crouched between the wheels of that chair. His habits, his way of living and dressing, his attachments to the local people, to the poor and needy, his affection for the young, never altered. A man of considerable wealth, he nevertheless continued in England to live alone, at first in a room in country pubs, later in the chauffeur's house as manager of his brother's farm at Castle Hill, and finally—still surrounded by the smell of horses, cattle and pigs—in a roadside cottage belonging to an ageing and devoted couple who fed and attended him to the end.

To every room he inhabited he gave the unmistakable stamp of his personality. Dark and reeking of shag, their peeling walls would be patched with faded photographs of horses and men in frames at tipsy angles. On what had once been a kitchen table stood stacks of yellowed newspapers, mouse-nibbled copies of magazines for the farmer and the cattle-breeder, pamphlets on artificial manure, prices on the Stock Exchange, and on top of this mass of paper a saddle, a hip-flask, a long-handled hunting-crop, a chipped mug, a rusty horseshoe, a discarded denture. Under the high brass bedstead and round the outskirts of the room piles of old books created tables for a wash-basin, a jug, a hairbrush, a cut-throat razor, a pair of enormous boots, a shoe-horn. And in the centre of the jumble, in a high-backed chair against a couple of torn cushions, beside him a packing-case with tobacco pouch, pipes, the dentures currently in use at meal-times, and the hand-mirror (for the purpose of watching, undaunted, the spread of the growth that was killing him), the cripple himself, the once tall Captain who, half a century before, had been engaged to marry the girl whose first child, by another captain, I became.

All her life, at the mention of his name, there came over my mother's face a certain look, a momentary closing of the eyes, a tightening of the thin lips, which privately I always called the 'I-refuse-to-think-of-it' look. Such was her character, such her Irish Protestant up-bringing, her horror of illness, her capacity for self-deception, that my mother was able not only to banish from her mind thoughts of 'unpleasant' events, she did in time actually convince herself, and sometimes even others, that they had 'never really happened'. And I often used to think what a thorn it must have been in her flesh that no matter where my parents chose to live, the rooms in which this man spent his life would invariably be close at hand.

During his last agonizing years he and my people were separated by no more than a mile of country road. After the second operation on the malignant cancer in the head, when he could no longer get into the wheel-chair, no longer stagger on crutches from his room, my wife and I would drive over to tea with my mother, and on our way home occasionally call in at the tiny cottage on the roadside.

Before leaving my mother's house: 'I think we'll just drop in on Uncle Jack,' I would say.

Whereupon the eyes closed, the lips tightened. She lowered her head. 'Give him my love,' she would almost whisper.

And once, when everyone knew the end was fast approaching, she said, she forced herself to ask: 'Do you think—do you think I ought to come with you?'

'I am sure he would like to see you,' I replied.

See, by then, was about all the wreck of a man could do. Out of one eye. For the other had been removed.

I will not relate what he looked like, how the grafted skin on the skull appeared in the dim light, how the room smelled. Nor attempt to describe, to imagine, what the ordeal of that visit—for him, for my mother—must have been like.

All the way home she remained silent. Then, at the door of her house: 'I am glad I went,' she said. And sighed.

Alopecia

FAY WELDON

IT'S 1972.

'Fiddlesticks,' says Maureen. Everyone else says 'crap' or 'balls', but Maureen's current gear, being Victorian sprigged muslin, demands an appropriate vocabulary. 'Fiddlesticks. If Erica says her bald patches are anything to do with Brian, she's lying. It's alopecia.'

'I wonder which would be worse,' murmurs Ruthie in her soft voice, 'to have a husband who tears your hair out in the night, or to have alopecia.'

Ruthie wears a black fringed satin dress exactly half a century old, through which, alas, Ruthie's ribs show even more prominently than her breasts. Ruthie's little girl Poppy (at three too old for playgroup, too young for school) wears a long white (well, yellowish) cotton shift which contrasts nicely with her mother's dusty black.

'At least the husband might improve, with effort,' says Alison, 'unlike alopecia. You wake up one morning with a single bald patch and a month or so later there you are, completely bald. Nothing anyone can do about it.' Alison, plump mother of three, sensibly wears a flowered Laura Ashley dress which hides her bulges.

'It might be quite interesting,' remarks Maureen. 'The egg-head approach. One would have to forgo the past, of course, and go all space-age, which would hardly be in keeping with the mood of the times.'

'You are the mood of the times, Maureen,' murmurs Ruthie, as expected. Ruthie's simple adulation of Maureen is both gratifying and embarrassing, everyone agrees.

Everyone agrees, on the other hand, that Erica Bisham of the bald patches is a stupid, if ladylike, bitch.

Maureen, Ruthie and Alison are working in Maureen's premises off the Kings Road. Here Maureen, as befits the glamour of her station, the initiator of Mauromania, meets the media, expresses opinions, answers the phone, dictates to secretaries (male), selects and matches fabrics, approves designs and makes, in general, multitudinous decisions—although not, perhaps, as multitudinous as the ones she was accustomed to make in the middle and late sixties, when the world was young and rich and wild. Maureen is forty but you'd never think it. She wears a large hat by day (and, one imagines, night) which shades her anxious face and guards her still pretty complexion. Maureen leads a rich life. Maureen once had her pubic hair dyed green to match her fingernails—or so her husband Kim announced to a waiting (well, such were the days) world: she divorced him not long after, having lost his baby at five months. The head of the foetus, rumour had it, emerged green, and her National Health Service GP refused to treat her any more, and she had to go private after all—she with her Marxist convictions.

That was 1968. If the state's going to tumble, let it tumble. The sooner the better. Drop out, everyone! Mauromania magnifique! And off goes Maureen's husband Kim with Maureen's *au pair*—a broad-hipped, big-bosomed girl, good breeding material, with an ordinary coarse and curly bush, if somewhat reddish.

Still, it had been a good marriage as marriages go. And as marriages go, it went. Or so Maureen remarked to the press, on her way home (six beds, six baths, four recep., American kitchen, patio, South Ken) from the divorce courts. Maureen cried a little in the taxi, when she'd left her public well behind, partly from shock and grief, mostly from confusion that beloved Kim, Kim, who so despised the nuclear family, who had so often said that he and she ought to get divorced in order to have a true and unfettered relationship, that Maureen's Kim should have speeded up Maureen's divorce in order to marry Maureen's *au pair* girl before the baby arrived. Kim and Maureen had been married for fifteen years. Kim had been Kevin from Liverpool before seeing the light or at any rate the guru. Maureen had always been just Maureen from Hoxton, east London: remained so through the birth, rise and triumph of Mauromania. It was her charm. Local girl makes good.

Maureen has experience of life: she knows by now it is wise to watch what people do, not listen to what they say. Well, it's something to have learned. Ruthie and Alison, her (nominal) partners from the beginning, each her junior by some ten years, listen to Maureen with respect and diffidence.

And should they not? After the green pubic hair episode, after the *au pair* and divorce incident, Maureen marries a swinging professor of philosophy, a miracle of charm and intelligence who appears on TV, a catch indeed. Maureen's knowledge of life and ideas is considerable: it must be: lying next to a man all night, every night, wouldn't you absorb something from him? Sop up some knowledge, some information, some wisdom?

Someone, somewhere, surely, must know everything? God help us if they don't.

Maureen and the professor have a son. He's dyslexic—the professor tries to teach him English at two, Latin at three, and Greek at four—and now, away at a special boarding-school, is doing well on the sports field and happy. She and the professor are divorced. He lives in the South Ken home, for reasons known only to lawyers. All Maureen wants now (she says, from her penthouse) is another chance: someone familiar, trustworthy, ordinary. A suburban house, a family, privacy, obscurity. To run Mauromania from a distance: delegating: dusting, only pausing to rake in the money.

Mauromania magnifique!

'Mind you,' says Maureen now, matching up purple feathers with emerald satin to great effect, 'if I was Brian I'd certainly beat Erica to death. Fancy having to listen to that whining voice night after night. The only trouble is he's become too much of a gentleman. He'll never have the courage to do it. Turned his back on his origins, and all that. It doesn't do.'

Maureen has known Brian since the old days in Hoxton. They were evacuees together: shared the same bomb shelter on their return from Starvation Hall in Ipswich—a boys' public school considered unsafe for the gentry's children but all right for the East Enders'. (The cooking staff nobly stayed on; but, distressingly, the boys, it seems, had been living on less than rations for generations, hence Starvation Hall.)

'It's all Erica's fantasy,' says Ruthie, knowledgeably. 'A kind of dreadful sexual fantasy. She *wants* him to beat her up so she trots round London saying he does. Poor Brian. It comes from marrying into the English upper classes, old style. She must be nearly fifty. She has this kind of battered-looking face.'

Her voice trails away. There is a slight pause in the conversation.

'Um,' says Alison.

'That's drink,' says Maureen, decisively. 'Poor bloody Brian. What a ball-breaker to have married.' Brian was Maureen's childhood sweetheart. What a romantic, platonic idyll! She nearly married him once, twice, three times. Once in the very early days, before Kim, before anyone, when Brian was selling books from a barrow in Hoxton market. Once again, after Kim and before the professor, by which time Brian was taking expensive photographs of the trendy and successful—only then Erica turned up in Brian's bed, long-legged, disdainful, beautiful, with a model's precise and organised face, and the fluty tones of the girl who'd bought her school uniform at Harrods, and that was the end of that. Not that Brian had ever exactly proposed to Maureen; not that they'd ever even been to bed together: they just knew each other and each other's bed partners so well that each knew what the other was thinking, feeling, hoping. Both from Hoxton, east London: Brian, Maureen; and a host of others, too. What was there, you might ask, about that particular acre of the East End which over a period of a few years gave birth to such a crop of remarkable children, such a flare-up of human creativity in terms of writing, painting, designing, entertaining? Changing the world? One might almost think God had chosen it for an experiment in intensive talent-breeding. Mauromania, God-sent.

And then there was another time in the late sixties, when there was a short break between Brian and Erica— Erica had a hysterectomy against Brian's wishes; but during those two weeks of opportunity Maureen, her business flourishing, her designs world-famous Mauromania a label for even trendy young queens (royal, that is) to boast, rich beyond counting—during those two special weeks of all weeks Maureen fell head over heels classically in love with Pedro: no, not a fisherman, but as good as—Italian, young, open-shirted, sloe-eyed, a designer. And Pedro, it later transpired, was using Maureen as a means to laying all the models, both male and female (Maureen had gone into menswear). Maureen was the last to know, and by the time she did Brian was in Erica's arms (or whatever) again. A sorry episode. Maureen spent six months at a health farm, on a diet of grapes and brown rice. At the end of that time Mauromania Man had collapsed, her business manager had jumped out of a tenth-floor window, and an employee's irate mother was bringing a criminal suit against Maureen personally for running a brothel. It was all quite irrational. If the employee, a runaway girl of, it turned out, only thirteen, but looking twenty, and an excellent seamstress, had contracted gonorrhoea whilst in her employ, was that Maureen's fault? The judge, sensibly, decided it wasn't, and that the entire collapse of British respectability could not fairly be laid at Maureen's door. Legal costs came to more than £12,000: the country house and stables had to be sold at a knockdown price. That was disaster year.

And who was there during that time to hold Maureen's hand? No one. Everyone, it seemed, had troubles enough of their own. And all the time, Maureen's poor heart bled for Pedro, of the ridiculous name and the sloe eyes, long departed, laughing, streptococci surging in his wake. And of all the old friends and allies only Ruthie and Alison lingered on, two familiar faces in a sea of changing ones, getting younger every day, and hungrier year by year not for fun, fashion, and excitement, but for money, promotion, security, and acknowledgement.

The staff even went on strike once, walking up and down outside the workshop with placards announcing hours and wages, backed by Maoists, women's liberationists and trade unionists, all vying for their trumpery allegiance, puffing up a tiny news story into a colossal media joke, not even bothering to get Maureen's side of the story—absenteeism, drug addiction, shoddy workmanship, falling markets, constricting profits.

But Ruthie gave birth to Poppy, unexpectedly, in the black and gold ladies' rest-room (customers only—just as well it wasn't in the staff toilets where the plaster was flaking and the old wall-cisterns came down on your head if you pulled the chain) and that cheered everyone up. Business perked up, staff calmed down as unemployment rose. Poppy, born of Mauromania, was everyone's favourite, everyone's mascot. Her father, only seventeen, was doing two years inside, framed by the police for dealing in pot. He did not have too bad a time—he got three A-levels and university entrance inside, which he would never have got outside, but it meant poor little Poppy had to do without a father's care and Ruthie had to cope on her own. Ruthie of the ribs.

Alison, meanwhile, somewhat apologetically, had married Hugo, a rather straight and respectable actor who believed in womens' rights; they had three children and lived in a cosy house with a garden in Muswell Hill: Alison even belonged to the PTA! Hugo was frequently without work, but Hugo and Alison manage, between them, to keep going and even happy. Hugo thinks Alison should ask for a rise, but Alison doesn't like to. That's the trouble about working for a friend and being only a nominal partner.

'Don't let's talk about Erica Bisham any more,' says Maureen now. 'It's too draggy a subject.' So they don't.

But one midnight a couple of weeks later, when Maureen, Ruthie and Alison are working late to meet an order—as is their frequent custom these days (and one most unnerving to Hugo, Alison's husband)—there comes a tap on the door. It's Erica, of course. Who else would tap, in such an ingratiating fashion? Others cry 'Hi!' or 'Peace!' and enter. Erica, smiling nervously and crookedly; her yellow hair eccentric in the extreme; bushy in places, sparse in others. Couldn't she wear a wig? She is wearing a Marks & Spencer nightie which not even Ruthie would think of wearing, in the house or out of it. It is bloodstained down the back. (Menstruation is not yet so fashionable as to be thus demonstrable, though it can be talked about at length.) A strong smell of what? alcohol, or is it nail-varnish? hangs about her. Drinking again. (Alison's husband, Hugo, in a long period of unemployment, once veered on to the edge of alcoholism but fortunately veered off again, and the smell of nail-varnish, acetone, gave a warning sign of an agitated, overworked liver, unable to cope with acetaldehyde, the highly toxic product of alcohol metabolism.)

'Could I sit down?' says Erica. 'He's locked me out. Am I speaking oddly? I think I've lost a tooth. I'm hurting under my ribs and I feel sick.'

They stare at her—this drunk, dishevelled, trouble-making woman.

'He,' says Maureen finally. 'Who's he?'

'Brian.'

'You're going to get into trouble, Erica,' says Ruthie, though more kindly than Maureen, 'if you go round saying dreadful things about poor Brian.'

'I wouldn't have come here if there was anywhere else,' says Erica.

'You must have friends,' observes Maureen, as if to say, Don't count us amongst them if you have.

'No.' Erica sounds desolate. 'He has his friends at work. I don't seem to have any.'

'I wonder why,' says Maureen under her breath; and then, 'I'll get you a taxi home, Erica. You're in no state to be out.'

'I'm not drunk, if that's what you think.'

'Who ever is,' sighs Ruthie, sewing relentlessly on. Four more blouses by one o'clock. Then, thank God, bed.

Little Poppy has passed out on a pile of orange ostrich feathers. She looks fantastic.

'If Brian does beat you up,' says Alison, who has seen her father beat her mother on many a Saturday night, 'why don't you go to the police?'

'I did once, and they told me to go home and behave myself.'

'Or leave him?' Alison's mother left Alison's father.

'Where would I go? How would I live? The children? I'm not well.' Erica sways. Alison puts a chair beneath her. Erica sits, legs planted wide apart, head down. A few drops of blood fall on the floor. From Erica's mouth, or elsewhere? Maureen doesn't see, doesn't care. Maureen's on the phone, calling radio cabs who do not reply.

'I try not to provoke him, but I never know what's going to set him off,' mumbles Erica. 'Tonight it was Tampax. He said only whores wore Tampax. He tore it out and kicked me. Look.'

Erica pulls up her nightie (Erica's wearing no knickers) and exposes her private parts in a most shameful, shameless fashion. The inner thighs are blue and mottled, but then, dear God, she's nearly fifty.

What does one look like, thigh-wise, nearing fifty? Maureen's the nearest to knowing, and she's not saying. As for Ruthie, she hopes she'll never get there. Fifty!

'The woman's mad,' mutters Maureen. 'Perhaps I'd better call the loony wagon, not a taxi?'

'Thank God Poppy's asleep.' Poor Ruthie seems in a state of shock.

'You can come home with me, Erica,' says Alison.

'God knows what Hugo will say. He hates matrimonial upsets. He says if you get in between, they both start hitting you.'

Erica gurgles, a kind of mirthless laugh. From behind her, mysteriously, a child steps out. She is eight, stocky, plain and pale, dressed in boring Ladybird pyjamas.

'Mummy?'

Erica's head whips up; the blood on Erica's lip is wiped away by the back of Erica's hand. Erica straightens her back. Erica smiles. Erica's voice is completely normal, ladylike.

'Hallo darling. How did you get here?'

'I followed you. Daddy was too angry.'

'He'll be better soon, Libby,' says Erica brightly. 'He always is.'

'We're not going home? Please don't let's go home. I don't want to see Daddy.'

'Bitch,' mutters Maureen, 'she's even turned his own child against him. Poor bloody Brian. There's nothing at all the matter with her. Look at her now.'

For Erica is on her feet, smoothing Libby's hair, murmuring, laughing.

'Poor bloody Erica,' observes Alison. It is the first time she has ever defied Maureen, let alone challenged her wisdom. And rising with as much dignity as her plump frame and flounced cotton will allow, Alison takes Erica and Libby home and installs them for the night in the spare room of the cosy house in Muswell Hill.

Hugo isn't any too pleased. 'Your smart sick friends,' he says. And, 'I'd beat a woman like that to death myself, any day.' And, 'Dragging that poor child into it: it's appalling.' He's nice to Libby, though, and rings up Brian to say she's safe and sound, and looks after her while Alison takes Erica round to the doctor. The doctor sends Erica round to the hospital, and the hospital admit her for tests and treatment.

'Why bother?' enquires Hugo. 'Everyone knows she's mad.'

In the evening, Brian comes all the way to Muswell Hill in his Ferrari to pick up Libby. He's an attractive man: intelligent and perspicacious, fatherly and gentle. Just right, it occurs to Alison, for Maureen.

'I'm so sorry about all this,' he says. 'I love my wife dearly but she has her problems. There's a dark side to her nature—you've no idea. A deep inner violence—which of course manifests itself in this kind of behaviour. She's deeply psychophrenic. I'm so afraid for the child.'

'The hospital did admit her,' murmurs Alison. 'And not to the psychiatric ward, but the surgical.'

'That will be her hysterectomy scar again,' says Brian. 'Any slight tussle—she goes quite wild, and I have to restrain her for her own safety—and it opens up. It's symptomatic of her inner sickness, I'm afraid. She even says herself it opens to let the build-up of wickedness out. What I can't forgive is the way she drags poor little Libby into things. She's turning the child against me. God knows what I'm going to do. Well, at least I can bury myself in work. I hear you're an actor, Hugo.'

Hugo offers Brian a drink, and Brian offers (well, more or less) Hugo a part in a new rock musical going on in the West End. Alison goes to visit Erica in hospital.

'Erica has some liver damage, but it's not irreversible: she'll be feeling nauseous for a couple of months, that's all. She's lost a back tooth and she's had a couple of stitches put in her vagina,' says Alison to Maureen and Ruthie next day. The blouse order never got completed— re-orders now look dubious. But if staff haven't the loyalty to work unpaid overtime any more, what else can be expected? The partners (nominal) can't do everything.

'Who said so?' enquires Maureen, sceptically. 'The hospital or Erica?'

'Well,' Alison is obliged to admit, 'Erica.'

'You are an innocent, Alison.' Maureen sounds quite cross. 'Erica can't open her poor sick mouth without uttering a lie. It's her hysterectomy scar opened up again, that's all. No wonder. She's a nymphomaniac: she doesn't leave Brian alone month in, month out. She has the soul of a whore. Poor man. He's so upset by it all. Who wouldn't be?'

Brian takes Maureen out to lunch. In the evening, Alison goes to visit Erica in hospital, but Erica has gone. Sister says, oh yes, her husband came to fetch her. They hadn't wanted to let her go so soon but Mr Bisham seemed such a sensible, loving man, they thought he could look after his wife perfectly well, and it's always nicer at home, isn't it? Was it *the* Brian Bisham? Yes, she'd thought so. Poor Mrs Bisham—what a dreadful world we live in, when a respectable married woman can't even walk the streets without being brutally attacked, sexually assaulted by strangers.

*

It's 1973.

Winter. A chill wind blowing, a colder one still to come. A three-day week imposed by an insane government. Strikes, power-cuts, black-outs. Maureen, Ruthie and Alison work by candlelight. All three wear fun-furs— old stock, unsaleable. Poppy is staying with Ruthie's mother, as she usually is these days. Poppy has been developing a squint, and the doctor says she has to wear glasses with one blanked-out lens for at least eighteen months. Ruthie, honestly, can't bear to see her daughter thus. Ruthie's mother, of a prosaic nature, a lady who buys her clothes at C & A Outsize, doesn't seem to mind.

'If oil prices go up,' says Maureen gloomily, 'what's going to happen to the price of synthetics? What's going to happen to Mauromania, come to that?'

'Go up the market,' says Alison, 'the rich are always with us.'

Maureen says nothing. Maureen is bad-tempered, these days. She is having some kind of painful trouble with her teeth, which she seems less well able to cope with than she can the trouble with staff (overpaid), raw materials (unavailable), delivery dates (impossible), distribution (unchancy), costs (soaring), profits (falling), re-investment (non-existent). And the snow has ruined the penthouse roof and it has to be replaced, at the cost of many thousands. Men friends come and go: they seem to get younger and less feeling. Sometimes Maureen feels they treat her as a joke. They ask her about the sixties as if it were a different age: of Mauromania as if it were something as dead as the dodo—but it's still surely a label which counts for something, brings in foreign currency, ought really to bring her some recognition. The Beatles got the MBE; why not Maureen of Mauromania? Throw-away clothes for throw-away people?

'Ruthie,' says Maureen. 'You're getting careless. You've put the pocket on upside-down, and it's going for copying. That's going to hold up the whole batch. Oh, what the hell. Let it go through.'

'Do you ever hear anything of Erica Bisham?' Ruthie asks Alison, more to annoy Maureen than because she wants to know. 'Is she still wandering round in the middle of the night?'

'Hugo does a lot of work for Brian, these days,' says Alison carefully. 'But he never mentions Erica.'

'Poor Brian. What a fate. A wife with alopecia! I expect she's bald as a coot by now. As good a revenge as any, I dare say.'

'It was nothing to do with alopecia,' says Alison. 'Brian just tore out chunks of her hair, nightly.' Alison's own marriage isn't going so well. Hugo's got the lead in one of Brian's long runs in the West End. Show business consumes his thoughts and ambitions. The ingenue lead is in love with Hugo and says so, on TV quiz games and in the Sunday supplements. She's under age. Alison feels old, bored and boring.

'These days I'd believe anything,' says Ruthie. 'She must provoke him dreadfully.'

'I don't know what you've got against Brian, Alison,' says Maureen. 'Perhaps you just don't like men. In which case you're not much good in a fashion house. Ruthie, that's another pocket upside-down.'

'I feel sick,' says Ruthie. Ruthie's pregnant again. Ruthie's husband was out of prison and with her for exactly two weeks; then he flew off to Istanbul to smuggle marijuana back into the country. He was caught. Now he languishes in a Turkish jail. 'What's to become of us?'

'We must develop a sense of sisterhood,' says Alison, 'that's all.'

It's 1974.

Alison's doorbell rings at three in the morning. It is election night, and Alison is watching the results on television. Hugo (presumably) is watching them somewhere else, with the ingenue lead—now above the age of consent, which spoils the pleasure somewhat. It is Erica and Libby. Erica's nose is broken. Libby, at ten, is now in charge. Both are in their night-clothes. Alison pays off the taxi-driver, who won't take a tip. 'What a world,' he says.

'I couldn't think where else to come,' says Libby. 'Where he wouldn't follow her. I wrote down this address last time I was here. I thought it might come in useful, sometime.'

It is the end of Alison's marriage, and the end of Alison's job. Hugo, whose future career largely depends on Brian's goodwill, says, you have Erica in the house or you have me. Alison says, I'll have Erica. 'Lesbian, dyke,' says Hugo, bitterly. 'Don't think you'll keep the children, you won't.'

Maureen says, 'That was the first and last time Brian ever hit her. He told me so. She lurched towards him on purpose. She *wanted* her nose broken; idiot Alison, don't you understand? Erica nags and provokes. She calls him dreadful, insulting, injuring things in public. She flays him with words. She says he's impotent: an artistic failure. I've heard her. Everyone has. When finally he lashes out, she's delighted. Her last husband beat hell out of her. She's a born victim.'

Alison takes Erica to a free solicitor, who—surprise, surprise—is efficient and who collects evidence and affidavits from doctors and hospitals all over London, has a restraining order issued against Brian, gets Libby and Erica back into the matrimonial home, and starts and completes divorce proceedings and gets handsome alimony. It all takes six weeks, at the end of which time Erica's face has altogether lost its battered look.

Alison turns up at work the morning after the alimony details are known and has the door shut in her face. Mauromania. The lettering is flaking. The door needs re-painting.

Hugo sells the house over Alison's head. By this time she and the children are living in a two-room flat.

Bad times.

'You're a very destructive person,' says Maureen to Alison in the letter officially terminating her appointment. 'Brian never did you any harm, and you've ruined his life, you've interfered in a marriage in a really wicked way. You've encouraged Brian's wife to break up his perfectly good marriage, and turned Brian's child against him, and not content with that you've crippled Brian financially. Erica would never have been so vindictive if she hadn't had you egging her on. It was you who made her go to law, and once things get into lawyers' hands they escalate, as who better than I should know? The law has nothing to do with natural justice, idiot Alison. Hugo is very concerned for you and thinks you should have mental treatment. As for me, I am really upset. I expected friendship and loyalty from you, Alison; I trained you and employed you, and saw you through good times and bad. I may say, too, that your notion of Mauromania becoming an exclusive fashion house, which I followed through for a time, was all but disastrous, and symptomatic of your general bad judgement. After all, this is the people's age, the sixties, the seventies, the eighties, right through to the new century. Brian is coming in with me in the new world Mauromania.'

Mauromania, meretricious!

A month or so later, Brian and Maureen are married. It's a terrific wedding, somewhat marred by the death of Ruthie—killed, with her new baby, in the Paris air crash, on her way home from Istanbul, where she'd been trying to get her young husband released from prison. She'd failed. But then, if she'd succeeded, he'd have been killed too, and he was too young to die. Little Poppy was at the memorial service, in a sensible trouser-suit from C & A, brought for her by Gran, without her glasses, both enormous eyes apparently now functioning well. She didn't remember Alison, who was standing next to her, crying softly. Soft beds of orange feathers, far away, another world.

Alison wasn't asked to the wedding, which in any case clashed with the mass funeral of the air-crash victims.

Just as well. What would she have worn?

It's 1975.

It's summer, long and hot. Alison walks past Mauromania. Alison has remarried. She is happy. She didn't
know that such ordinary everyday kindness could
exist and endure. Alison is wearing, like everyone else,
jeans and a T-shirt. A new ordinariness, a common sense,
a serio-cheerfulness infuses the times. Female breasts
swing free, libertarian by day, erotic by night, costing
nobody anything, or at most a little modesty. No profit
there.

Mauromania is derelict, boarded up. A barrow outside
is piled with old stock, sale-priced. Coloured tights,
fun-furs, feathers, slinky dresses. Passers-by pick over
the stuff, occasionally buy, mostly look, and giggle, and
mourn, and remember.

Alison, watching, sees Maureen coming down the steps.
Maureen is rather nastily dressed in a bright yellow
silk shift. Maureen's hair seems strange, bushy in parts,
sparse in others. Maureen has abandoned her hat. Maureen
bends over the barrow, and Alison can see the bald
patches on her scalp.

'Alopecia,' says Alison, out loud. Maureen looks up.
Maureen's face seems somehow worn and battered, and
old and haunted beyond its years. Maureen stares at
Alison, recognising, and Maureen's face takes on an
expression of half-apology, half-entreaty. Maureen wants
to speak.

But Alison only smiles brightly and lightly and walks
on.

'I'm afraid poor Maureen has alopecia, on top of everything else,' she says to anyone who happens to enquire after that sad, forgotten figure, who once had everything—except, perhaps, a sense of sisterhood.